Did You Get One of THESE Yet Today?

Autoworker Tales - Stories, Legends, and Slightly Embellished Truths

Brandy Booth

Catalyst Publishing

Contributors

Cover art by Jason Nuttall and Libby Booth

Edited by George Mason and John Chavez

Disclaimer

This book is a work of fiction and is intended for entertainment purposes only.

Unless otherwise indicated, all names, characters, businesses, places, events and incidents in this book are either the product of the author's imagination or used in a fictitious manner.

Any resemblance to actual persons, living or dead, or actual events is purely coincidental.

Do not do, say, or think of doing anything you read in this book.

If you are incapable of knowing the difference between a good idea and a bad one, READ SOMETHING ELSE!

This book is intended for persons 18 years of age and older.

That means to read it, you MUST be an adult and are therefore – by law – responsible for your own actions.

Thanks for reading.

For Tom, Don, Dick, Russ, and Jackie -

Tom was the guy who first popped the question.

Don was my mentor.

Dick told the first stories I remember.

Russ broke me in – much to the dismay of those around us.

And without Jackie, I wouldn't be an autoworker – or on this planet - at all.

Contents

Introduction   VI

1. They're Just Car Parts   1

2. Best Job in the Plant   22

3. Messin' with the Boss   52

4. Fighting Like Brothers and Sisters   97

5. Overboard Paybacks   123

6. That's Bound to Leave a Mark!   150

7. Horseplay   198

Want More?   223

Share the Laughs   224

101 Ways to Pop the Question   226

Where to Next?   237

Introduction

• • • ● • ● ● • • •

There's no other greeting quite like it.

Like some things in life, it feels awkward at first but becomes rather enjoyable as you do it more often.

The moment the old autoworker hit me with his signature salute in early September of 2012 is a day I'll remember forever.

Even though I'd been around industrial jokesters for nearly 20 years by that point in time, it was still surprising when the old boy popped the question that day.

Some might have taken offense to his antics and avoided him.

Not me.

I couldn't get back to talk to him fast enough.

He'd flipped us an insider's hello – an authentic signal to come share stories with him and to hear his.

It's with an outstretched arm and an inverted fist that I joyfully extend the same invitation to you.

Near the end of the book, you'll find a section titled "101 Ways to Pop the Question" that culminates with an invitation to share your own ideas so you might someday see them in print.

The pages between these and those include many of the stories I've seen, heard, or thought about over a thirty year stretch in various automotive factories.

NO SHORTAGE OF CHARACTERS

Looking back, I realize I caught the tail-end of an incredible era by hiring into the auto industry in the early nineties.

There was something significant about the people who had worked in auto factories during the industry's heydays of the sixties and seventies.

The folks produced by that era were every bit as authentic as the classic cars and trucks that came rolling off the assembly lines back then.

I'm not sure if it was because they were close to retirement and didn't worry about getting in trouble, or if they were just losing their minds, but some of the things they got away with are almost unthinkable in today's world.

And from what I could tell, a switch really did flip in some of their heads the moment they punched into work that turned them into somebody else.

There's no way they could have been the same person at home.

For example, I met sweet little grannies who swore like sailors if you got in their way as they moved tons of steel with huge fork trucks and overhead cranes.

Their grandkids would look at them a lot differently if they'd seen the way Nana wrestled those controls when big loads were trying to get away.

Just as I started getting used to that group of people, the industry began to evolve.

In the late nineties, retirements and flowbacks caused people to move from factory to factory in search of a new home.

I'm convinced that at least a few of these "gypsies" moved from place to place because they kept getting in trouble everywhere they went, and the system kept scooting them along instead of dealing with their nonsense.

Some of the best stories ever told resulted from two random crazies butting heads as they crossed paths on their career journey across America.

Between these unbalanced folk and the professional jokesters that seemed strategically sprinkled throughout every plant, you never knew what to expect on any given day.

Twelve hour shifts seven days a week produced some high-quality pranksters who went to great lengths to "pull one over" on the boss or an unsuspecting coworker.

As you'll find out, nobody – not even the plant manager – was off limits.

NO DIRT. NO DISRESPECT.

The auto industry and the people associated with it are sometimes cast in a negative light due to circumstances both within and outside of their control.

While there's never a shortage of negative things to focus on in any industry, that's not the intent of this book.

You won't find any company, union, or people bashing here.

This book is a collection of stories meant to make you laugh, share some lingo, and give you a peek into how a day in the life of an autoworker might compare to yours.

Most of these stories are funny, but some will come off as confrontational, awkward, or even downright shocking.

But again - they're not mean or disrespectful toward anyone.

I have the utmost respect for the hard-working folks I work with, the company that employs us, the union that represents us, and even the poor boss who has the unfortunate job of telling me what to do every day.

I'm just a storyteller, and I like funny things.

BUT ARE THEY TRUE?

From time to time, someone will try to pin me down as to whether a certain story is true or not.

"Of course, you changed the names," they say.

"But did this actually happen? Are these stories true?"

Aside from the legal disclaimer and the words "slightly embellished" in the subtitle, I'll say this:

Whether or not these stories are true completely depends on YOU.

If you're the type of person who thinks autoworkers are just lazy, overpaid reasons why cars cost so much, then...

I made it all up.

Every word.

I invented these people, stories, and situations in my head as I hammered out thousands of high-quality auto parts at a time and wrote my ideas down when I got home.

But if you're someone who enjoys funny work stories and isn't looking to start trouble, then... well...

Aw, heck.

This intro is long enough.

Let's get to the good stuff.

Chapter One

They're Just Car Parts

If you want to push management over the edge when they're cranked up about broken machines, excessive scrap, or other production losses, look 'em dead in the eye and say: "I don't know what you're upset about. They're just car parts."

Works every time.

The Shower Jumper

The first time it happened, I didn't know what to do.

I wasn't sure if I should run, try to shove him and then run, or act like nothing was happening.

I looked over at the others.

Nobody seemed alarmed.

In fact, nobody was paying attention to him at all.

Yet there he was.

Not three feet in front of me, a heavily tattooed, bald, naked man in his fifties was jumping up and down, shaking wildly while growling through the verses of a popular Madonna song.

Water was spraying.

Junk was flying.

It was unforgettable.

I was stunned, like a kid who had fallen off the monkey bars.

"Had I done something to cause this?" I wondered.

"Am I going to have to naked-fight a crazy guy in a dirty locker room on my first day in a new plant?"

I was struggling not to look at him (which would have directly violated the unwritten "No Eye-Contact" rule that exists in every men's shower room in the world), but he had my full attention.

"Why is he right next to me?"

Even though he wasn't touching me, he HAD to know this was a violation of my personal space.

"Is he trying to intimidate me? Nah, he isn't directly facing me."

"Did I accidentally stare at him in the shower while trying to remember my grocery list?"

"DEAR GOD! WHY IS THIS HAPPENING?!?"

My mind was racing, but my body was frozen in place.

Fifteen seconds ago, everything had seemed normal.

I'd exited the shower room and grabbed my towel off the hook.

As I began to dry off, this fella strolled out of the shower room, marched past me, and turned to face the bench.

But the instant his shower tray touched down, he spun 180 degrees, crouched, and exploded into the air with a nasally yell that caught me off guard and scared the heck out of me.

I'd instinctively thrown up a forearm block that I tried to play off as an extra toweling off motion when I realized he wasn't coming at me.

"Was this really happening?" I thought, as I slowly looked around.

I spotted Jake (the other new apprentice) through the shower room door just as he noticed the bouncing bald guy.

(Jake was shy and hadn't seemed comfortable with a bunch of grimy factory workers in the musty old shower room, even before this happened.)

When Jake saw the Shower Jumper, his jaw dropped, and his face froze that way.

Shampoo was running down the side of his head into his eyes and mouth, but he was in shock and couldn't move.

At least now I knew I wasn't crazy. But what the heck was going on here?

The Shower Jumper's feet pounded the rubber mat like a boxer's fists on a side of beef.

His guttural groans shoved out explicit lyrics in (what I was certain was) the wrong order.

Since he seemed to be staying in place, I took a step back and began to lower my guard.

This made no sense at all.

He'd seemed normal enough in the dimly lit open-stall shower room.

He was a wiry little guy, about 5'-7", and fairly fit for an autoworker of his age.

It had occurred to me he might have been talking to himself when I first walked in, but I didn't think much of it.

I'd met a lot of colorful characters in the last 20 months or so, but this was a situation of a whole different nature.

"In your face" didn't even begin to describe it.

It wasn't easy to keep my composure as the Shower Jumper's ballet dragged on for what seemed like hours but was probably only three or four minutes.

The whole experience was off.

DID YOU GET ONE OF THESE YET TODAY?

It made no sense that he was singing the song he was singing, nor that he'd slowed it down and was growling through the verses in a low, heavy voice.

His jumping was out-of-time with his singing, yet neither matched the sound his arms, legs, and other flapping appendages made as they collided under the orange glow of the heat lamp.

"Why Madonna? Why choose this time and place to express yourself?"

"Wait, did he just change songs?"

"Really? Like a virgin? I don't think so."

I was too stunned to even contemplate why he was doing what he was doing.

The only thing I knew for sure was I wanted to get out of there.

I took two steps out into the locker room, and I realized I'd forgotten the tray that holds my toothbrush, soap, and shampoo on the bench near the heat lamp.

I turned back around and nearly got knocked over by Jake, who was on a mission to put some serious distance between himself and the Shower Jumper.

He still had shampoo in his hair as he came flying past me, and he hadn't bothered to dry off at all. He'd just snatched his towel off the hook and made a run for his locker.

But as he tried rounding the corner, his left flip-flop blew a strap and squirted out from under his foot on the slippery tile, sending him crashing into the row of lockers on the wall.

He scrambled to regain his balance and limped around the corner and out of sight.

A couple of guys standing by their lockers snickered as I retrieved my tray.

As I bent down to pick it up, the Shower Jumper abruptly stopped, inhaled and exhaled loudly, picked up his tray, and marched past without acknowledging me at all.

And at that moment, it dawned on me why he did what he did.

He didn't have a towel.

I found out later that he *never* brought a towel.

For 13 years at that plant, the man showered every day but never used a towel.

After he showered, he jumped on the mat under the heat lamp to dry off.

He repeated this routine every day.

It didn't matter who was in there.

This was HIS stage, and he owned that piece of real estate from the time he stepped out of the shower until the moment he decided the show was over.

Everybody knew it, and nobody said a word.

Any new people who didn't know it and got too close to the heat lamp at the wrong time received the same rude awakening as me.

DID YOU GET ONE OF THESE YET TODAY?

When I got to school that evening, the other apprentices who had been to that plant were itching to ask me the question.

"Hey Booth, you shower before you go home, don't you?"

Five heads whipped around, and I couldn't keep a straight face.

All I could do was look down, bite my lip, and shake my head.

"You've seen it too, huh? He's pretty, um..." I stumbled.

I couldn't think of an appropriate word to describe what I'd seen, and nobody offered anything to help me, so I just put my head in my hands, rubbed my eyes, and sighed.

"You can't unsee things," I said to nobody in particular.

"What did he sing?" they all wanted to know.

When I told them it was a combination of Madonna tunes, over half of them had been right.

After all, they said he had Madonna posters and cutouts in his locker, at his workstation, on top of his toolbox, and peppered around all the other places he spent time.

He'd told some of them he'd been to several of her concerts and would love to be a backup dancer for one of her performances.

A few guys were disappointed that he hadn't cut loose with the Danzig song he did pretty well, or the George Michael number that would even make a room full of fully clothed guys uncomfortable.

(For the record, I saw both of these catchy little performances at a later date - still against my will, but from a safer distance.)

THE SECRET CODE

I ducked into a break area one day, threw a bag with a bar burger and fries into the microwave, pushed "88" on the timer, and hit "Start".

A guy sitting at the picnic table looked at me funny and asked why I pushed 88 seconds instead of a minute and 28 seconds.

"Wouldn't it be the same?" he inquired.

"Not at all," I said in a low tone as I put my hands on the table in front of him.

His skeptical look told me I'd have to slow-play this if I was going to sell it.

I glanced at the microwave and leaned in closer.

"Have you heard about the 'crispy' feature on the newer microwaves?" I asked.

When he said he hadn't, I explained that the microwave companies had invented a solution to the soggy food problem but couldn't tell people yet because of a lawsuit with the toaster oven industry.

As a result, a secret feature was added that emits a different type of convection heat that makes food crispy instead of soggy.

"It's only available on certain models, and this happens to be one of them," I declared.

Right on cue, the timer beeped, and I pulled out my food and had him try a French fry.

"See what I mean?"

"Yeah, that's a HUGE difference!" he exclaimed.

(In his defense, the fries from the bar across the road were super crispy by nature.)

A few days later, I walked into the same break room just in time to hear a girl ask her friend if she thought it would work on pizza.

"Do I have to leave it in the full 88 seconds?" she inquired. "My piece isn't that big."

"I wouldn't think so," the other girl replied. It's dry heat on that setting. I don't think the length of time matters."

"Just if you're cooking something bigger, you'd have to put it on 88 seconds and restart it on 88 seconds again to get the dry heat again."

I walked out of that break area smiling from ear to ear.

My work here was done!

ALMOST HAD IT

Clint Enos went out for lunch every Tuesday evening to buy a lottery ticket, a Mountain Dew, and a sub sandwich from the little deli down the road from the plant.

He'd been playing the same numbers (his wife and kids' birth dates) every Tuesday for almost a decade, keeping the same draw slip in the top of his toolbox to take with him each week.

One Tuesday, five minutes before lunch, a critical overhead line broke and management needed everyone to respond immediately to get it fixed.

Clint had been ready to go out the door when the call went out, but the boss walked by as the "line down" alarm went off, so he jumped on his cart and answered the call.

We finished the job around 9 pm and went back to the millwright area to put our stuff away.

While we were cleaning up, Clint's wife started paging him nonstop, so he ran to use the phone in the office to see what the emergency was.

When he came out, he looked physically injured and was white as a ghost.

We were all certain that someone had died, so we sat back and hung our heads and offered support if he needed anything.

And then, without warning, the man went off like a rocket.

We watched in amazement as he emptied his tool bag on the bed of the cart and threw every tool he owned against the far wall, teaching me some new phrases along the way.

As he threw the bag and kicked the cart, we all became certain that his wife had cheated on him, or he found out his daughter was pregnant by the bad kid in town.

But then he started saying "F*<k this job!" and "Stupid broken overhead!"

And almost as fast as his fit had started, it stopped, and he broke down sobbing.

DID YOU GET ONE OF THESE YET TODAY?

"Clint, what's going on? Are you ok?" Our leader asked, as Clint hung his head.

"I almost made it out the door," he muttered to himself.

"Clint? What's wrong?" the leader asked again.

But Clint was locked up tight and didn't seem to be able to talk.

He grabbed his lunch box, snapped the lock on his toolbox, and walked out the door.

We knew it was something serious.

It wasn't even time to go home yet.

He never picked up any of the tools he threw.

He just left.

Clint took vacation the rest of that week, and he let management know he wouldn't be coming in for any of the overtime between Christmas and New Year that year, which was extremely uncommon for this overtime hound.

We found out a few days later that every one of his numbers had hit - even the kicker - and he'd missed out on over 4 million dollars.

None of us had thought about it being Tuesday.

Clint returned to work after New Year's and eased back into his Tuesday routine.

But he did say he was picking new numbers because he didn't think the other ones would hit again.

PENNY FOR YOUR...THOUGHTS?

Tim Shefler built a drip pan to be installed underneath a machine, and Burt Labowski was on his hands and knees welding it up.

Like always, about three inches of Burt's sweaty butt crack was sticking out the top of his pants.

When I came to see if Shef needed help moving the pan into place, he pulled a handful of change out of his pocket.

"Who carries that much change?" I asked, as Shef put a finger to his lips.

"That would totally pull my pants down or fall out of my coverall pockets," I said in a low voice.

Shef didn't answer.

He just kept fishing through the pile in his hand.

And then, one by one, he casually started dropping pennies down Burt's butt crack.

He got six in before Burt finished the stick of rod he was burning and dabbed at his exposed crack with his thick leather welder's glove.

"It's too hot for this shit," he said under his breath as he dropped his hood and started his final rod.

Shef put five more in before he ran out of pennies - or Burt ran out of rod – I forget which happened first.

"I think the reason it works so good is because they're warm from being in my pocket," Shef quietly coached. "Don't try it if they're cold, Kid."

As Burt finished his seam and started wrapping up his leads, a penny came out of his pant leg and rolled across the floor.

He didn't notice.

A few hours later, I'd nearly forgotten about the incident until I was getting ready to take a shower in the locker room.

From two rows over, I could hear the "ting ting ting" of pennies hitting the floor and I heard Burt say, "What the??!!?" Then, "Sonofabitch!!!"

Now, trust me - I try not to look at guys in the shower, but I had to laugh when he showed up in the open-stalled shower room with pennies stuck in his butt crack.

It happened again a week later, this time with little washers from the crib.

"They won't even use real money anymore," Burt whined.

THE NO-LOOK GRAB

Every week when Randy "Tubby" Rhineheart wiped his machines down, Frankie Ford would sneak up close behind him and say, "Hey Tubby, when you're finished with that, I've got a big black truck in the parking lot you can rub on next."

Sometimes he'd say it in a sultry voice in Tubby's ear and pretend to rub up against him.

Frankie kept his area clean, but he didn't wipe his machines down like Tubby did.

"One of these times you're going to startle me," Tubby warned. "Then you'll have the bull by the horn, or vice versa."

One day, a factory guy (outside machine builder) was training their group to run a new-style grinder that had just been installed.

The factory guy wanted a white board to draw some diagrams, but they didn't have one, so Tubby suggested they wipe down the side of the machine and use a dry erase marker.

The factory guy liked that idea.

Tubby went to get a rag and spray bottle as the others started filtering in from lunch.

As he started wiping down the machine, a voice behind him said, "Hey, when you're done with that, I've got a..."

Tubby cut him off loudly and said, "Let me guess...a big black..." and he spun around super-fast with the rag in his hand, reaching low as he spun because Frankie was super short.

To his absolute horror, there stood the plant manager with a surprised look on his face and Tubby's outstretched hand three inches from his crotch.

Everyone in the group let out a gasp and Tubby's eyes got really wide.

It was Frankie who broke the silence.

"Hey Tubby. We usually just shake hands around here."

"I... thought you... were... Frankie," he squeaked as he slowly pulled back his hand, never breaking eye contact.

"He's always sneaking up behind me and telling me to rub his big black..."

He shot a side-eyed glance at Frankie.

"Tell him, Frankie!" Tubby begged.

"Hey, it's your story," Frankie shrugged. "Tell it any way you want."

Tubby looked down at the floor and wished he was someplace else.

"It's okay. I get it," the plant manager said, as he shook his head and backed away.

PARTNERS FOR LIFE

Craig Wonch and Billy Perrow lived forty minutes from the plant and rode to work together nearly every day.

Craig and Billy were jokesters who liked to have fun at other people's expense.

Once in a while, those 'other people' would pay them back.

One snowy Friday in January, they left work and headed toward home.

As they pulled up to a stoplight in the first small town north of the plant, they heard a bunch of honking and cheering, but they didn't know why.

"Someone must be celebrating," Billy said as they drove away.

Little did they know that someone at work had put a "Just Married" sign on the back of their car and tied a bunch of milk jugs and tin cans on two ropes behind them.

Because it was winter and there was fresh snow on the roads, they couldn't hear the junk they were dragging.

They got honked at twice in the next town, and a carload of teenagers drove next to them for a few miles, laughing and waving.

They both agreed that something was odd, but neither figured it out.

They made it all the way to their hometown and stopped for a beer before a local walked into the bar, pointed at them, and told the bartender he wanted to buy the newlyweds a drink.

SCREW YOUR BOOTS!

Andy Carrier was due for a new pair of boots.

The guys had been ribbing him about his steel toes looking like they were going to fall out, but he liked the old boots he'd gotten from the company store.

To be honest, a lot of people wore those same boots and hung on to them for a long time because they wore in so comfortably.

One day, a pair of the same type of boots as Andy wore was sitting in the top of a garbage can near the millwright area.

They were the same color and had the same issue with the steel toes looking like they were trying to escape.

"I've got an idea," said Brad Porter, as we finished bolting down a stand.

"Grab those boots and follow me," he said.

I grabbed the boots and trailed behind as he carried the roto-hammer through the millwright shop to the row of toolboxes and footlockers along the back wall.

Brad set the drill down on the table by Andy's box, grabbed Andy's footlocker, and shoved it to the side.

Andy had left early that day, and his boots always sat on the concrete floor underneath his footlocker.

Brad picked up Andy's boots and stashed them in an empty cabinet near the bench.

"Give me those boots," Brad ordered.

I smiled as he drilled two holes in the soles and placed the boots where Andy's normally sat.

He pushed the drill inside the holes in the soles and marked two spots on the floor.

Then he picked the boots up, drilled two holes in the floor, and swept up the dust.

He pulled two anchor bolts out of his pocket, pushed them through the soles, and proceeded to bolt the boots to the floor.

The next morning when Andy came to work, he leaned down to grab the boots to put them on.

He almost pulled himself off balance as they refused to move from their spot.

He tugged at them again, but they weren't coming out without a fight.

He shoved his footlocker out of the way and gave them a good yank.

When they still didn't break free, he turned toward the table, gave us all a grin, and unlocked his toolbox to get out a hammer and deck chisel.

Apparently, he thought the trickster had glued them to the floor with spray glue.

As you and I both know, that wasn't the case.

When he started to drive the chisel under the first boot, he spotted the bolt and his face dropped with disappointment.

He grabbed a ratchet, socket, and extension and unbolted his boots.

"Look, I know I needed new boots, but you guys know we don't mess around with people's personal belongings."

I thought he did a pretty good job of keeping his cool as he looked through the hole in the bottom.

(This would have ticked me off had someone done it to me.)

While Andy wasn't about to yell or swear, he wasn't above grumbling about having to go to the shoe store at a different plant or spending money before he'd wanted to.

Just before he was going to leave, Brad came strolling by and opened the cabinet with Andy's unharmed boots inside.

Gotcha.

THE NEAR MISS

John Stone was in heaven.

He'd never eaten authentic Mexican food before, and he was hooked from the first bite.

"Try some jalapeños," Jose Murillo said, as he pushed the jar of sliced peppers toward the skinny white fella.

"I'd better not," John held up his hand. "I've never been a fan of hot peppers."

"Jalapeños aren't that hot," Murillo chided.

"But stay away from that jug of hot sauce and that plate of habaneros."

"Maybe I'll try just one..." John Stone decided, as he put a small piece of jalapeño on the end of his enchilada and took a bite.

"Wow! That's got great flavor!" he said, as he put on four more and wolfed it down.

He ate three or four small tacos with jalapeños on them, and he even tried a dash of hot sauce on a chip before our crew went back to work after lunch.

A few hours later, I was on my way home from work when I almost got wrecked.

I'd been driving in the left-hand lane on the expressway when a maroon truck with a matching topper came across all three lanes, jammed on the brakes inches in front of me, and slid sideways into the "Authorized Vehicles Only" access in the median.

I braked hard and yanked the wheel to avoid hitting him and ended up spraying gravel all over, nearly side-swiping another vehicle as I swerved back onto the freeway.

The whole thing happened so fast that I didn't have time to cuss him out until I'd gotten back out on the road.

I tried to look in my rear-view mirror to see if he had crashed, but I was shaken up and needed to focus on where I was going.

I'd forgotten all about it by the next morning when John came rushing up to me.

"Hey Kid. I'm sorry I almost wrecked you yesterday!" he apologized.

"That was you in the maroon truck? What the heck were you thinking?" I asked in disbelief.

John Stone was always so calm, cool, and collected. He was one of the best heavy equipment operators in the plant. This didn't make sense to me.

"Man, I felt terrible. I saw you almost crash into the median. I didn't realize I was that close."

"What made you cut across three lanes of traffic?" I asked again.

He looked down at the ground and back up at me with sad, bloodshot eyes.

"I was on top of the bridge when my gut started rumbling. Those peppers hit me hard! By the time I got to the bottom, I knew I had to get someplace FAST."

He motioned to the right as he continued, "I started to get off on the interchange, but there's no bathroom even close to it for miles. The I looked across the median and saw the rest area. That's when I almost hit you."

"Did you make it?" I immediately had to know.

"Yeah, but it wasn't a pretty sight when I got there," he winced.

"The guy in the stall next to me must have thought I was dying. I was all sweaty and sliding around, making noises that would give people nightmares."

"It burned so bad I thought about putting the seat up and dipping my butt in the water."

"Man, I'm glad we didn't crash then," I said, as I slapped him on the shoulder.

"That would have been one ugly accident scene."

Chapter Two

Best Job in the Plant

• • • ● ● ● ● ● • •

"Nothing moves without a millwright, Kid," Charlie Sagebrush said, as I drove the 30,000-pound Taylor "Big Red" diesel fork truck out the back door of the plant and headed for the Prototype Center.

"This is the best job in the plant," the old journeyman assured me.

From what I could tell so far, he was right.

The millwright trade was the absolute best.

I'd only been at my job a few months, but I'd already operated a 50-ton overhead crane that spanned the highbay, a man lift that reached 100+ feet in the air, and mobile cranes of every shape and size.

I learned to run Drotts, Brodersons, Groves, Hysters, Condors, Genies, JLGs, Clarks, Yales, Taylors, and a goofy looking "crane car" that had previously been used to unload railroad cars.

For a farm kid who liked driving big things, this job was a dream.

The metal working tools were ridiculously big as well.

I'd operated a six-foot blowtorch, a shear that cut humongous plates of steel, and an upright bandsaw that sliced through huge blocks of metal like butter.

It was as if I'd landed in the middle of an oversized erector set and had the keys to everything I saw.

We'd built enormous mezzanines that hung from the roof steel, "flown" massive bull gears in and out of presses, and lifted exhaust fans the size of buses onto the roof of the plant.

But on this day, we were headed for a job that still ranks as one of the coolest demolition jobs I've ever done.

THE COOLEST DEMO JOB EVER

I let off the throttle as we crossed the old railroad tracks between the plants so the bumps didn't beat us up too badly.

It was a nice day in late September, and this part of the complex was new to me.

As we approached our destination, I was told to wait on the truck while Charlie went in the office to find out exactly what they needed us to do.

He was looking at a sheet of paper as he came walking out, and he folded it and shoved it into his breast pocket as he climbed onto the big forklift.

"My turn to drive, Kid," he announced, and I slid out of the driver's seat and sat on the ledge next to him.

The big truck growled as he disengaged the brake and started off toward the job.

We rounded the corner behind the offices and drove down a narrow lane into the area where prototype vehicles were stored.

The whole left side of the roadway was lined with new vehicles of all makes and models.

I didn't recognize some of the names of the cars because our company had joint ventures in other countries.

We turned one more corner and saw four vehicles sitting a couple car lengths away from the rest along some concrete barriers.

There was a full-size Chevy extended cab truck, a Jeep Grand Cherokee, a Cadillac Sedan Deville, and a Chevy Caprice.

"Hang on, Kid," Sagebrush said, as he gunned the throttle and sped down the drive toward the cars.

At first, I was confused, as there didn't appear to be anything that needed to be moved by our big red fork truck.

But my confusion turned to alarm as I realized we were headed straight toward the side of the Cadillac, and Charlie had no intention of stopping.

He lifted the forks a couple feet off the ground just before impact, and our fork tips speared both doors of the new white Cadillac, shoving the car sideways into the Caprice.

"We're going to get fired," I thought to myself, as the forks blew through the opposite doors and the mast slammed into the side of the car.

My jaw was in my lap and my eyes were as big as watermelons as Charlie revved up the engine and raised the car high into the air.

Even back then, this had to be a $30-$40,000 vehicle.

He jammed it into reverse, tilted the forks forward, and spun the wheel all the way to the left.

As we gained momentum, the car shot off our forks and landed on its side up against the concrete barriers.

I searched Charlie's face for answers, but all I could see was an ear-to-ear grin.

This old boy was in full demolition mode.

It took a moment to lower his forks level with the exposed engine and transmission, but when they reached the right height, he shoved it into gear and skewered the drivetrain hard enough to move the huge highway barrier at least a foot.

"Has he completely lost his mind?" I wondered, as he picked it up again.

My mind was racing like never before.

He snagged the front bumper and spun the car so it was perpendicular to the barrier, lowered his forks to the ground, and proceeded to drive straight into it the long way.

The back popped up and over the barrier, almost sending the whole car over the top.

He slammed on the brakes and stopped before our forks touched the concrete.

I looked over at the two big fork dents in the side of the Caprice.

This was insane.

I thought about my '81 Monte Carlo sitting in the parking lot.

"We have to completely destroy these vehicles before they leave the site," Sagebrush informed me. "There can't be anything left."

"I don't understand," I said in a feeble voice.

"These are test cars that have been fitted with prototype parts," he explained. "If anyone were to drive these in public and someone was hurt, the liability would be astronomical."

"But why can't they just put the original parts back on and sell them at a discount," I argued, still not fully grasping the logic.

"They all get destroyed," he said flatly.

"Why don't they have them crushed?" I inquired.

"They're headed for the crusher after they leave here," he said, in a matter-of-fact tone. "But there can't be anything left to salvage."

And we made sure of that.

Sagebrush finished off the Cadillac and destroyed the Caprice.

"Those two are all yours," he smiled, as he pointed to the truck and the Jeep.

I got a sick feeling in the pit of my stomach when I looked at the dark blue 4x4.

This was my dream truck (color and all), and even with this good job, it would be a long time before I'd be able to afford one.

Couldn't we just swap this with my Monte and call it a day?

"Get after it, Kid, there's a semi and a 40-foot trailer coming in half an hour," he ordered, as he hopped off the truck and went to talk to a guy who'd came to watch.

I almost cried as I speared the Chevy's driver's door and the cab behind it.

That new car smell filled my nostrils as the opposite door flew open.

Glass shattered, and the front tire blew as I smashed it into the barrier.

"Screw it," I thought, as I lifted it all the way up and tilted my forks forward.

I cranked the wheel off, shifted it into reverse, and put the pedal to the metal, just as I'd seen Charlie do.

As the truck slid off the forks and landed on its side, I heard Sagebrush holler.

I slammed on the brakes and stopped just inches away from a Corvette that was parked at the end of the long row of cars.

I hadn't been paying attention to the back of the truck and had gotten a little wide in my turn.

"Not that one," he yelled. "They're not done playing with that one yet!"

I pummeled the truck until Sagebrush told me to go after the Jeep.

Both vehicles appeared loaded to me.

I made short work of the Jeep, except I had a hard time getting the tires to blow.

Those buggers just wouldn't give in.

I finally stuck a fork in just the right place to finish the job.

The semi pulled in, and we stacked the wreckage two high and sent them off to the boneyard.

As I watched the semi driver pull away, I knew I'd never forget the day we wrecked more than a hundred grand worth of vehicles in less than an hour.

THE DIRECT HIT

There were six factories at the main complex (and one across town) that produced the components needed to make a complete steering system.

Since apprentices needed to be proficient at working on the equipment in all the plants, they spent a year or so at their home plant, then "rotated" around the other plants every six to eight months after that.

With a week to go in this plant, it was time to start saying goodbye.

Around 8 am on Monday morning, I was standing next to a pipefitter apprentice when two journeyman fitters came walking up.

The taller one had a six-foot piece of four-inch pvc pipe with a cap on one end slung over his shoulder.

"So, it's your last week, huh," the shorter one asked the apprentice standing next to me.

"Yup. Time to move, I guess," he replied.

Without warning, the tall guy tipped the plastic pipe forward, and at least two gallons of water shot out and hit the apprentice squarely in the chest.

I jumped back and waited for him to lose his cool.

He slowly lifted his arm to see if there was a dry spot left to wipe the water from the side of his face.

"I thought apprentices got wet on their last day in the plant," he groaned.

"We like to celebrate our apprentices for a full week around here," the shorter guy chuckled.

"It's because we like you," the taller one said. "If we didn't like you, we wouldn't bother to get you wet. We'd just be glad when you were gone."

"That one's called the Direct Hit," the shorter guy said.

"It's called that because you stand right in front of the guy and make eye contact as you make your hit."

"Get it? Direct... Hit..."

"Yes, I figured that out," the dripping apprentice nodded.

"Booth is going to be soaked," he added, as he eyed me up. "I heard the millwrights talking about how much fun they're going to have drowning you."

I knew he was telling the truth.

I'd heard a couple of them talking about how fun it is to "water" the apprentices when the committee had announced rotation a few weeks before.

"It helps them grow into better journeymen," one had said.

When the millwrights heard the pipefitters had gotten their apprentice wet, they wouldn't settle for being outdone.

It was only a matter of time.

MISTAKEN IDENTITY

The next day, I was heading up the stairs to the bathroom above the maintenance area to do my morning business when I noticed Paul Krause spying on me from behind a toolbox.

Paul was a journeyman millwright who I'd worked with a few times.

He'd made it known to everyone that he was going to get me wet.

I pretended not to see him as I reached the landing and turned the corner into the bathroom.

As I passed by the janitor's closet before the first stall, I spotted the metal bucket full of water that had been pre-staged next to the back wall.

A quick peek through the crack in the wall verified what I'd already known.

Paul was on a dead run for the stairs leading up to the bathroom.

I had to act fast.

I thought about grabbing the bucket and drowning him as he rounded the corner, but instead I spun around and ran to the ladder that led to the roof hatch.

There was one door closed in the row of eight stalls, and it wasn't near the ladder, so I wouldn't bother the guy by climbing up.

Because it was August, the hatch was already open, and I escaped without a sound.

By this time, I really had to go, so I trotted across the roof to the stairs leading down to the men's locker room and took care of my business there.

When I came down from the locker room and crossed the aisle leading back to the maintenance area, I could hear Rocky (the maintenance leader) yelling from a hundred yards away.

"YOU STUPID SONOFA…" Rocky wailed.

He'd been reading his morning paper in his favorite stall when three gallons of water hit him squarely in the chest.

Paul knew he'd screwed up and had tried to get away clean, but Rocky spotted him through a crack in the wall at the back of his stall.

Now Paul was getting reamed out good.

"But I thought you were the apprentice," he pleaded.

Rocky's combover hung limply to the wrong side as the puddle of water at his feet grew larger.

Both men turned to mean-mug me as I shuffled past, whistling softly with my head down.

(I wasn't stopping to talk!)

The rest of the crew was laughing and picking on them for being outsmarted by an apprentice as I jumped on my cart and headed for my job.

I knew I was in for it now.

ISOLATED SHOWERS

To my amazement, nobody threw water for a couple of days after Rocky took my hit.

I don't know if they were too embarrassed to try again or if they were just mad at me, but things were far too quiet.

Nevertheless, I walked around like a scared rabbit all week.

By the time Friday rolled around, I thought about dumping a bucket of water over my own head just to break the tension.

I soon found out that wouldn't be necessary.

As I approached the chair where I changed into my work boots every morning, I could tell something wasn't right.

All the guys who normally sat in the chairs next to my toolbox were standing in a group by the coffeepot, and they stopped talking and looked my way as I bent down to get my boots.

Because their chairs were empty, I decided to sit in a different one facing the coffeepot while I put my boots on.

I slowly scanned the guys by the coffeepot, but nobody was running at me with a bucket.

They'd gone back to talking amongst themselves when I happened to look up above my chair.

High in the rafters, I could see a bright yellow electrical cord attached to a valve on the end of a new chunk of pipe.

The cord ran across the truss toward the coffeepot and down the column in the middle of the group.

Just then, a big guy named Jerry Shoultes turned the corner from the other direction and came walking toward his toolbox.

"Mornin', Kid," he said, as he went past.

I looked back down at my boot laces as I returned his greeting, and he spun, snatched me in a bear hug, and dragged me into my chair.

"DO IT NOW!!!" he yelled.

As he pinned me in the chair, a giant burst of water came shooting down from the open ASCO valve and drenched us both like the factory rats we were.

Although they didn't get the drop on me, I still learned a lot that day.

I learned about electronically controlled water valves, setting traps on the off shift, and taking one for the team.

A DOZEN THUMBS UP!

"In thirty years, your hands will look just like mine, Kid," Herb Verlenbeck said.

He held his mangled mitts up like a surgeon, and the other journeymen in our huddle began to laugh.

I tried not to stare, but I did notice that none of his fingers appeared to be straight, and at least two didn't have a nail.

(I'd later learn that one was gone at the second knuckle.)

"Don't listen to Snuffy, Kid," another journeyman said. "He's makes bad choices with his appendages."

"Plus, he's slow and clumsy," another added.

"C'mon Kid. I don't have to take this. Let's go," Herb said.

It didn't take long to figure out why the crew had nicknamed him "Snuffy".

His big brown eyes and low, nasally voice sounded just like the big brown mammoth from Sesame Street named Snuffleupagus.

But Herb Verlenbeck was an easy guy to work with and learn from. He didn't get excited about anything, and he seemed to be a bit of a perfectionist.

After working with Snuffy a couple of days, I started to notice a few quirky things about the way he did certain jobs.

For one, the big lefty had a habit of searching the rack for exactly the right piece of steel, like a picky guy selecting a piece of lumber from the bottom of the pile in a home improvement store.

Once he figured out which piece he wanted (they all looked the same to me), he'd lay an end on the bench and look down the edge, like he was sighting down the barrel of a gun.

If it wasn't exactly right, he'd get out his three-pound sledgehammer and beat on it until he thought it was straight enough to use.

I'd watched him go through this ritual one morning, and I wondered why it mattered if the whole piece was straight if we only needed a couple feet.

I didn't say anything though.

Herb had taught me not to second-guess him on a similar job a few days earlier.

I watched in silence as he laid the ten-foot piece of two-inch angle on the edge of the table and reached for his trusty sledge.

Just as he went to whack it, the piece slipped off the edge.

He attempted to shove it back into place mid-swing, but his plan went terribly wrong.

As the angle iron fell to the floor, I watched in horror as the big hammer came down and smashed the guts out of Herb's right thumb.

The sickening "thud" was followed by a high-pitched squeal, and he grabbed his forearm and spun around in a circle before leaning against the table to keep from falling down.

"Don't take your glove off, Snuffy," said the guy working on the next bench over.

"Get on my cart and I'll take you to medical," the younger man offered.

My stomach was queasy from the thought of what must be going on inside his glove, and I slumped against a toolbox to regroup as they took off down the aisle.

Another millwright could see I was a few shades lighter than normal, and he invited me to take a ride out back for some fresh air.

After I gathered my wits (it took a while), we went to see if Herb was ok.

When we looked through the door into medical, we could see him sitting in a chair holding his bandaged thumb high in the air.

A pile of bloody gauze sat on a tray in front of him, and the nurse was wiping the counter down with a bottle of soapy bleach water.

Judging by the size of the wrap on his injured digit, we figured she must have used a whole roll of gauze on the poor schmuck's thumb.

"C'mon, Kid," my replacement journeyman said, and we climbed back on his cart.

We drove back to the department, and he wasted no time informing the other millwrights of Snuffy's condition.

Herb came back a few minutes before break, and the whole crew was standing around talking football.

"You alright, Snuffy?" they asked, as he approached the big circle with his hands in his pockets.

"Yeah, it's just a scratch," he said in a tough-guy voice.

"Let's see it," an older guy said.

"There's really not much to see," he explained, as he pulled his hand from his pocket and stuck out his gaudy white bandage.

In one synchronized motion, eleven right hands came out of pockets, each sporting a ridiculously oversized white bandage job on the thumb.

His jaw dropped, and he let out a little groan and slapped his forehead.

Then he started laughing, shook his head, and walked toward the coffeepot.

THE WETTEST I'VE EVER BEEN

When it came time to rotate out, I discovered the millwrights in this plant weren't as interested in throwing water as the ones at the last plant had been.

But the pipefitters in this plant more than made up the difference, as I found out almost a full month before I left.

I was hauling a container of scrap with a fork truck one Friday afternoon, and I spotted two guys with buckets on the roof in the bubble mirror as I approached the back door.

They'd warned me earlier that day they'd get me, and they weren't wasting any time.

I slammed the truck into reverse as my forks crossed through the doorway, and two buckets of water came raining down and harmlessly washed the bin I was hauling.

"HA! Missed me!" I thought, as I proceeded through the doorway.

Knowing their buckets were empty, I laughed out loud as I looked up to see who had tried to get me wet.

I'd guessed correctly that the two high seniority pipefitters working on my job were the culprits, and I looked up and gave them a cocky salute as I started to drive away.

As I turned back around, a one-inch stream of water hit me just in front of my right ear, blowing the hat and safety glasses clean off my head.

I hunkered down and tried to drive away, but the person directing the stream coming out the hole in the adjacent building had a deadly aim, and I got soaked down good.

"Dang pipefitters," I thought, as my truck bounced over the unevenly patched concrete.

The fitters in that plant were a tight-knit group, and they'd all taken the next day off to go tubing down a local river, then have a cookout at one guy's house.

I'd been invited to go, but chose to work instead.

I told them I'd be at their barbecue after work though.

They weren't off the river when I arrived at the guy's house, so I drove to the campground where they were expected to land and sat on a picnic table to wait.

As I looked around, I noticed a garden hose lying on the ground next to a tree by the river that was connected to a spigot not far away.

Just then, I saw tubes coming down the river and spotted the three guys who had soaked me down the day before floating along, drinking beer and chatting as their trip neared the end.

I turned on the water, kinked off the hose, and hid behind a tree.

When they were a few feet away, I stepped out from behind the tree and washed them down good.

One guy had just lit a cigarette, and I put it out like Smoky the Bear on caffeine.

I laughed as I shut the water off, and they shrugged and took their medicine like men.

We had a great time that night, eating, drinking, and enjoying each other's company.

I left relatively early because I was scheduled to work the next day.

My millwright crew was doing a tear-out in a department that could only be done on the weekend, and I was using a blowtorch to cut overhead steel down that had been used to support the ductwork for the old equipment.

I'd just finished the last cut before break and raised my shield so I could grab the controls and lower myself back down.

Halfway to the ground, the lift stopped moving.

As I looked around to see why my Genie no longer worked, I spotted a person standing next to the ground controls.

He'd pushed the e-stop, leaving me stranded fifteen feet in the air with no way to get down.

My heart dropped as I realized it was one of the guys I'd soaked down the day before.

As I started to squirm, I heard laughter from all around.

"I thought you guys had the day off," I laughed nervously, as I spotted the others.

I had no idea that all three of them had been scheduled to work Sunday.

They hadn't said a word when I told them I was leaving the party early because I was working the next day.

They just showed up on my job in payback mode.

As I looked around, I realized all three were holding one inch (or bigger) water hoses they'd unwrapped from the columns in the department where I was working.

The first stream of water knocked my hard hat, shield, safety glasses, and welder's cap off my head.

After that, there was so much water coming at me that I couldn't tell whose stream did what.

I tried my best to cover my face and ears as the high-pressure hoses pushed water into all my cracks and crevices.

Even though I still had thick leather welder's gloves on, I simply didn't have enough hands to cover all my orifices.

I've never been so wet in all my life, not before or since.

When the streams stopped, I started to uncover my face, and they hit me again for good measure.

"Don't mess with the fitters, Kid," my journeyman advised as I was finally allowed to come down.

He was right. These guys were expert-level water throwers, and I was out of my league.

I stayed moist for most of that month, but I never returned fire on them again.

I CUT IT THREE TIMES AND IT'S STILL TOO SHORT!

During the peak of the automotive industry, people were hired who hadn't finished high school.

A few of these folks couldn't read or write too well.

Rumor had it, one guy couldn't even sign his own name.

Ralphie Bills was an old pig farmer from a small town about forty minutes east of the plant.

Although he wasn't the smartest guy in any given room, he was a hard worker.

Because of that positive trait, the guys didn't mess with him as badly as they could have.

But they DID mess with him.

One day, Ralphie was sent to replace a discharge belt on an annealer.

The thick rubber belt was three feet wide and nearly forty feet long.

Ralphie pulled the old belt out and laid it on the floor along the aisle.

Because the new belting was on a big roll in the tool crib across the plant, he would have to measure and cut a new one.

The problem was, Ralphie didn't know how to read a measuring tape.

Brad Porter and Tim Shefler watched as Ralphie unscrewed the handle from a push broom and walked to one end of the belt.

He laid the broomstick on the floor, lined an end up with the end of the belt, and flipped it eight times until he reached the other end.

He marked the extra length of belt on the broomstick and wrote a number eight next to it.

Then he rolled up the old belt and threw it in the dumpster next to the aisle.

By this time, Ralphie was late for break.

He left the broomstick leaning against the end of the annealer and hopped on his cart to get a coffee.

Brad and Tim looked at each other and made a beeline for the broomstick.

They took it to the maintenance area, cut nearly three inches off with the bandsaw, and rounded it off with the belt sander.

Then they rubbed the end around on the dirty floor to make sure it looked just perfect and hurried to put it back where Ralphie had left it.

When break was over, Ralphie pulled up on his cart, grabbed the broomstick, and headed off to the tool crib.

He came back twenty minutes later with the new length of belt he'd cut and laced on the machine at the back of the crib.

Brad and Tim watched from behind some dunnage as Ralphie threaded the big belt back through the guides.

Once both sides were done, he grabbed both ends and pulled as hard as he could.

With nearly two feet left to go, the belt stopped coming together.

He ran to one end and looked underneath, feeling certain that it must be caught on something.

When he didn't find anything, he ran to the other end and went through the same motions again.

His pace slowed a little as he walked back to the center and grabbed ahold of the laced ends again.

He scratched his head and clamped on his belt stretching tool to hold it in place while he checked the take-ups.

He re-traced the path of the belt around the drive and tensioners.

This made no sense.

He was sure he'd measured right.

If anything, this belt should have been too long, as the old belt was likely stretched from a constant flow of heavy parts.

But it wasn't too long.

It was two feet too short.

In the end, Ralphie had to go back to the crib and make a two-foot splice to fill the gap.

(Note: I don't condone messing with folks – especially disadvantaged ones - but I do enjoy sharing stories about what I saw.)

THREE MEN IN A TRUCK

From time to time, maintenance crews were sent from the main complex to work at our sister plant across town.

The pickup trucks they rode in were extended cabs, but there wasn't a lot of leg room in the back, especially for burly maintenance men.

Most of the time, guys piled three-wide in the front seat to make the twenty-minute trip.

One day, John Stone, Andy Carrier, and Burt Labowski were assigned to the plant across town.

Andy didn't like to drive, and he didn't like to sit in the middle.

Because Burt didn't want to drive either, John Stone took the wheel.

Burt slid into the middle spot, and the three were on their way.

45

The sister plant was less than ten miles away, but the route was right through the busiest part of town, and there were a million stoplights.

As they rolled up to a red light at a busy intersection, Andy bent down and pretended to tie his shoe, making it appear that Burt was slid over next to John in a truck with only two men.

He stayed bent over for the duration of the light, but his coworkers didn't realize what he was doing.

As they came to the next red light, he bent over again.

This time, they pulled up next to two attractive young ladies making a left turn in a convertible in the next lane.

When one of the girls did a double take at the two men sitting so close to one another, Burt realized what Andy was up to.

He grabbed Andy by the arm and tried to haul him upright, but Andy was strong enough to hold his position, even though he was laughing so hard he almost couldn't breathe.

Much to Burt's dismay, Andy did this at every stoplight across town that day.

John didn't seem too bothered by Andy's game, but Burt was riled right up by the time they arrived at their destination.

He never let Andy put him in that position again, even opting for the back seat on the ride back to the plant.

Andy had fun with that joke while riding with different crew members, but it didn't take long before people were wise to his game and made him ride in the middle.

GOOD FOR ANOTHER HUNDRED THOUSAND

On my first day in a new plant, I watched an old biker enter the turnstile carrying a car tire under his arm.

He walked down the main aisle toward the back of the plant and stashed the tire under a bench in the millwright area.

When first break came, he pulled the tire out, raised the guard on the bandsaw, and cut it into quarters.

Then he cut the sidewalls off, leaving four sections of flat tread, each about a foot long.

Next, he laid a piece of cardboard on the floor to stand on and took his boots off.

He set the boots on the sections of tire and traced around them with a white paint pen.

He put them back on, lowered the guard on the bandsaw, and cut around the lines he'd traced.

Before he left that day, he cleaned the soles of his boots, sprayed them down with spray glue, put blocks of metal inside, and set them on the rubber cutouts.

"Good for another hundred thousand," he smiled. "Plus, I've got a spare set for when these wear out."

The more I got to know Bobby Grant, the more I came to understand he'd made some life choices that didn't leave him with much money at the end of the week.

KEEPING THE BOYS WARM

When January rolled around, Bobby's old Chevy van died.

He found a different motor, but it would take a week or more to install it, so he had to ride his old Harley to work.

I felt bad for him, but he lived twenty miles south of the plant, and I lived forty miles north.

There was no possible way I could give him a ride, and nobody else lived near him.

As luck would have it, temps dropped into the teens that week, but he had no choice but to tough it out.

On the coldest morning, I rounded the corner near his toolbox and something wet and furry brushed against my arm.

It startled me, and I jumped back to take a better look.

His coat and chaps were hanging where they usually were, but halfway down the mountain of leather was a big hunk of stinky brown fur.

As I slowly reached for the leg to see what the heck was going on, he saw me and came running up.

"I was freezing my nuts off last night on my way home, and the guy in front of me hit a deer," he explained.

"Not only did I get back straps out of the deal, but I also cut the hide off, salted it down, tanned it in my oven, and sewed it into the crotch of my leathers."

"My ride in was a lot warmer this morning."

Cameras weren't common in those days, but man do I ever wish I'd have taken a picture of Bobby Grant wearing those chaps!

MILLWRIGHT MOON PARADE

One hot Friday afternoon, our nine-man millwright crew completed a press rebuild that we'd worked twelve hours a day on for over two months.

We were finally getting a weekend off, and the crew was wound up.

As we loaded our rigging and got on our carts to leave, Rob Robeson realized he was the odd man out.

With only three flatbeds (the front one was a four-man carrier), there was no seat left, so he jumped on the front cart and hung on to the seat backs where Charlie Sagebrush and Larry Shoultes were sitting.

Rob had stripped off his swampy coveralls, exposing his gym shorts, cowboy boots, and a tee shirt that was a size and a half too small.

This was a sight to see, as Rob stood about six-three and weighed well over three hundred and fifty pounds.

His belly escaped from underneath his shirt as he leaned ahead to hang onto Charlie and Larry's seat, and we started down the aisle toward the back of the plant.

"We're outta here!" Rob exclaimed with a huge grin and a salute to the big press.

49

As we approached the plant's two main assembly lines, Charlie and Larry grabbed Rob by the arms and yanked him forward, pulling him off balance while pinning his chest into the metal wall that supported their seat backs.

Like lightning, Bobby Grant sprang from his seat and yanked Rob's running shorts and underwear down to his ankles, stripping him naked from tee shirt to boots.

The guys on the carts behind us started honking and yelling as we approached the assembly lines, and forty unsuspecting spectators looked our way.

I hadn't realized what was happening, and I turned to see what was going on.

"DON'T LOOK, KID," a voice from behind me yelled.

But it was too late.

Just three feet in front of me was Rob Robeson's big sweaty ass dancing around as he fought to get his arms free.

Although Rob was by far the strongest man on our crew, he was off-balance and in a very compromising position.

He really wanted to pull his shorts up, but Charlie and Jerry were hanging on with everything they had.

Our cart was heading straight for a building column, but neither man let go.

Just before impact, one of the guys up front managed to use their knee or foot to turn us, sending us careening back out into the aisle.

DID YOU GET ONE OF THESE YET TODAY?

The people on the lines had pulled the cords to stop production, and I could hear them whistling, laughing, and cheering over the "line down" music.

It was an instant party.

I'm embarrassed to say that I looked at Rob Robeson's big bare butt at least three times that day.

The first time was out of curiosity.

The second time was out of disbelief that he was still bottomless as we passed through the entire assembly area.

The third time was to make sure he didn't fall off the cart as Jerry finally let go to steer us around the corner that led to the back door.

This left Rob and Charlie wrestling, laughing, and swearing.

It took far too long for Rob to pull his drawers up that day.

And it's a memory that's forever burned into my brain, although it's been over twenty-five years ago.

I know there are people who worked in that factory who have Rob's biscuits (or worse) permanently burned into a dark recess in their minds.

After all, you can't unsee things.

Chapter Three

Messin' with the Boss

Ninety percent of the bosses in the auto industry are good people.

You'll find the other ten percent in the pages that follow.

HOLD THE APPLAUSE

The stage was set.

The auditorium was full.

The bigwigs from corporate were there.

This was the conference they'd all been waiting for.

Bonuses would be decided by the numbers released here.

Row upon row of "Best of the Best" trophies lined the front tables.

Performance-based promotions would be announced in the weeks to follow.

Plant managers from ten different factories were flanked by their teams.

Superintendents, supervisors, and high performers lined the rows.

The lights were dimmed, and the projector lit up the wall.

A young superintendent stepped up to the podium.

The site manager's photo filled the big screen.

His introduction was executed flawlessly.

Nearing the end, he jumped to his feet.

The auditorium burst into applause.

And the whole room went dark.

"The bulb must have blown," said a voice from the back.

A young supervisor rushed to the light switch.

Three minions scrambled to examine the overhead projector.

"It doesn't look like the bulb is blown. I'm not sure what happened," one said.

"The power is on, but it won't power back up until the bulb cools down," another added.

One of the plant managers sent a runner to retrieve another projector from his plant.

As the crowd started to stir, one superintendent began fanning the bulb with a file folder.

Soon, there were three people fanning the projector from all sides.

After ten minutes of this, the projector beeped, and the light came back on.

The lights were dimmed again, and the emcee bumbled his way through the lines he'd nailed so perfectly the first time.

The site manager stumbled on a cord as he approached the podium, but he caught himself and raised his arms to show he was ok.

The crowd let out a laugh and clapped and cheered.

And once again, the room went dark.

Groans and sighs filled the room as the lights came back on.

The bigwigs from corporate looked less than impressed.

"It must be a loose wire," said a voice in the back.

"My guy should be right back with the other projector," the plant manager said.

Ten minutes later, the runner returned with the replacement projector.

It took another ten minutes to swap them out, and they were ready to give it another try.

By now, the presentation was nearly 45 minutes behind schedule.

This would set the whole day back, including the plant tours and this evening's dinner.

When the replacement projector finally beeped and lit up the wall, the crowd clapped and cheered.

And just like before, the projector went dead.

One of the superintendents began tracing the power cord from the projector to the power supply located under the podium.

And that's where he found "The Clapper".

To this day, anytime I hear someone say, "Please hold the applause until the end", I remember the day a Clapper delayed an executive-level meeting for over an hour.

EASY FOR YOU TO SAY

Frankie Ford was a little biker fellow with a beard like a garden gnome and an attitude the size of Texas.

He was good at making car parts, and even better at poking fun at management.

Frankie came to work one morning and found that none of the machines in his department were running.

He put on his boots, grabbed a coffee, and set out to see what was going on.

There was a maintenance tag and a red lock on the main journal grinder that said, "Bad Valve, Part On Order", along with the third shift maintenance leader's name.

He looked the machine over but couldn't tell what had been pulled apart.

(If this machine was down, it meant Frankie wouldn't be able to run any parts, as this was the only journal grinder in the department.)

Because he didn't want to be "farmed out" to sort parts in a different department, Frankie filled a mop bucket and headed to an area that needed to be mopped.

About an hour into the shift, Cletus Grant came rushing up and demanded to know why Frankie wasn't running production.

"They didn't tell you? The journal grinder went down on third shift," Frankie said.

"The tag on the panel said a part is on order."

"What part?" Cletus wanted to know.

"Huh?"

"What part is maintenance waiting on?" Cletus demanded.

"I don't know," Frankie shrugged. "Some kind of valve. I'm not trades. I don't know anything about fixing machines."

"Well, if you see trades around that machine, ask them what they're waiting on."

Before Frankie could reply, Cletus spun around and rushed away down the aisle.

Frankie finished mopping and began wiping some of the dirty machines down with degreaser.

About twenty minutes later, two pipefitters came rolling up on a flatbed cart.

"How's it going?" Frankie asked.

"Great," they laughed. "We've been playing hide and seek with your boss. He keeps calling us on the radio, too, but we don't report to him. What a jackass."

They went on to explain that a check valve had gone bad in the grinder's control module on third shift, and they expected to have one within the hour.

They'd left their pager number at the shipping dock and were waiting on the page.

"Cletus has been chasing us around the plant, but we've been dodging him. He tried flagging us down and we acted like we didn't see or hear him. It was fun."

"We almost let him catch up to us at the tool crib, but we slipped down the side aisle at the last moment. He's been running a lot this morning."

Frankie nodded and smiled. "Well, he can use the exercise."

It pleased Frankie to know Cletus was being harassed in this manner.

Cletus's bulb was undoubtedly dim, but he could be a persistent pain in the butt if you didn't know how to throw him off your trail.

Just then, Frankie spotted Cletus running down the aisle toward them.

"Here he comes," he said from the corner of his mouth.

"Later," the fitters said in unison, as they took off down the back aisle.

Cletus yelled for them to stop but came up about a hundred yards short.

He was out of breath when he reached Frankie.

"What did they say," he gasped, hands resting on his knees.

His belly sloshed back and forth as he struggled to catch his breath.

"They said they're waiting for the part to arrive at shipping, and they'll put it right in."

"What part are they waiting for?" Cletus asked. "That's what I need to know."

"They said it's an air valve in the controller," Frankie replied.

"What's the valve called?" Cletus demanded.

"I'm not sure they ever said the name," Frankie said.

"I know you know the name of that valve!" Cletus growled, catching Frankie off-guard.

Frankie hesitated, then said, "Cletus, why is the name of the valve so important? The fitters are waiting for a page from shipping. When it comes in, they'll pick it up, install it, and I'll run production, because THAT'S my job."

"Look, Ford. I've got a meeting at 8 am, and I need to know the name of that valve so my bosses know I'm on top of this situation," Cletus hissed.

"Now I know you're just messing with me," he continued. "You know the name of that valve. You been around here long enough you can probably work on the machines better than trades can. Now stop bullshitting me. What is the name of that valve?"

Frankie scratched his head.

"You know, now that you mention it, I think I did hear one of the fitters say what kind of valve it was."

He tapped his forehead as if to jog his memory, and said, "It's a canooten valve."

"A what?" Cletus stumbled, as he looked up from his notepad.

"A canooten valve. It's the check valve inside the machine controller," Frankie nodded.

"A canooten valve? Are you sure? Do you know how to spell that?" He asked.

"C-A-N-O-O-T-E-N"

Cletus closed the notebook, looked at his watch, realized he was late, and bolted down the aisle toward the front of the plant.

About a half hour later, the assistant plant manager and the head engineer came down the aisle into Frankie's area.

The part had arrived and was being installed as they walked up.

"Canooten valve, huh? Nice," the engineer said with a grin.

"Hey, he kept asking me maintenance questions. I told him I'm no good at maintenance," Frankie shrugged.

"Well, he knows you tricked him now. A lot of people started laughing at him, but not until he'd said it into the microphone three times. The maintenance superintendent corrected him and reported the part had just hit the dock."

"It's all good," Frankie said with a smile.

And it was.

"SANDWICH, ANYONE?"

A couple weeks went by, and Cletus was still mad at Frankie for embarrassing him.

He'd been riding him ever since, threatening to write him up if he was caught screwing off.

DID YOU GET ONE OF THESE YET TODAY?

Frankie wasn't lazy, but he wasn't about to put up with Cletus's nonsense, either.

One morning, a machine in Frankie's area was up for a wheel change, so he dove right in and got it done.

Break was over by the time he got it back together, but the wheels needed to warm up for ten minutes, so he headed into the break area to cool off.

He bought a pop and a candy bar and sat down at a table next to a few skilled tradesmen.

The moment Frankie sat down, Cletus came busting through the door, slammed his handheld radio and clipboard on the table in front of him, and snarled, "I told you I was going to write you up for screwing off! Your ass is mine, now!"

"But he just got here..." said one skilled tradesman.

Frankie turned toward the tradesman, held up his hand, then turned back toward Cletus.

"What's the problem, Cletus?"

"What's the problem? I'll tell you what the problem is! It's after break and you haven't ran one goddamned part, and you're sitting in here! That's my problem!" Cletus screamed.

Frankie shrugged. "Blame it on third shift. When I got here, the wheel on the main grinder needed changing. I worked through break to get it back online."

"You're lying!" Cletus accused.

"NO, HE'S NOT," boomed Charlie Sagebrush.

The room went quiet at the senior tradesman's tone.

"Frankie just came in and sat down. Look at him. He's dripping with sweat from fixing your machine. The same wheel change takes eight hours on the off shift! Now leave him alone and drag your ass!" Sagebrush scolded.

Another tradesman added, "Cletus, had you gone to your department one time in the first three hours of the shift, you'd know what was going on!"

Cletus wasn't having any of this nonsense.

He spun and ran out the door, leaving his radio and clipboard in the middle of the table.

"Cletus Grant, Cletus Grant," the radio crackled.

Frankie stood from his chair, fished a handful of change from his pocket, and snatched the radio from the table.

He walked ten paces, turned, and squared off with the "Wheel of Death" (also known as the sandwich machine).

One by one in rapid-fire fashion, eleven quarters hit their mark.

He spun the wheel to roast beef and Swiss, slid the door open, grabbed the sandwich, crammed the little radio into the dispenser hole where the sandwich had been, and slammed the door shut.

Then he pushed the button to spin the wheel so the radio was in the back, and turned back toward the table.

"I didn't really want a sandwich," he said to the tradesmen. "They're not very good."

"But I'll bet this one tastes better than the others," he laughed, as he walked out the door.

It didn't take long for Cletus to come back through looking for his radio and clipboard.

He scooped up the clipboard and looked around.

"Where's my radio? C'mon guys. Stop screwing around. I know you have my radio."

The tradesmen looked down into their coffee, not saying a word.

"I'm not kidding! I have a meeting at ten o'clock," he chirped.

They still didn't say anything.

He opened his mouth again, but one of the tradesmen cut him off and said, "Hey guys? Do you hear something?"

From inside the sandwich machine, you could faintly hear "Cletus Grant. Cletus Grant."

At first, he thought someone had thrown the radio behind the machine.

But as it continued to squawk, he spotted it through the machine and spun the wheel around.

He tried to slide the door open at least three times with a puzzled look on his face.

When it dawned on him that he'd have to pay to get it out, he whirled around to see who was eating a sandwich.

"Stupid Frankie," he wailed as he dug out his wallet.

"Do you guys have any change?"

Of course, they told him they didn't.

He ran out of the room and returned five minutes later.

"You're going to be late for your meeting," one tradesman chided.

Cletus's hands were shaking as he inserted the coins, but he pushed the buttons and retrieved his radio without any further problems.

He grabbed an envelope from the end of the row of machines and filled it out for a refund.

Frankie later convinced the vending machine guy to give him the envelope.

I read it one day while it was hanging in Frankie's locker.

(He said he planned to frame it and put it on the wall in his garage when he retired.)

It has Cletus's signature below a sentence saying, "Someone put my radio in your sandwich machine - so I had to buy it back."

"It's not everyday you get an autographed summary of your pranks that's not on a discipline sheet," Frankie said.

Although Cletus left the company a long time ago, that envelope hangs in Frankie Ford's locker to this day.

THE LEAKY HIGH HORSE

"Whose bike is that?" Frankie wondered, as he wheeled into the parking lot.

He pulled into the motorcycle parking and walked to the far end to check out the new iron.

Frankie had only seen a couple trikes with matching sidecars, but none were as pretty as this one.

This pearl white Harley Davidson had more chrome than Frankie had ever seen on one machine.

His jaw dropped when he spotted the white leather streamers flowing from the edges of the seat, from the saddlebags, and off the ends of the handlebars.

There was only one person this pearly pile of rubber, rawhide, and steel could belong to, Frankie decided.

This was Walt King's new ride.

Walt was the third shift production boss in the department where Frankie worked.

Walt King could have been the poster boy for anyone's 'bulldog' package - round face and belly, bald head, thick lamb chop beard, handlebar mustache, and bushy eyebrows with beady eyes peering out from underneath.

The people who thought he looked mean were right.

Walt King was a jerk to work for, manipulating overtime and job assignments so nobody in Frankie's department wanted to come in early.

The other managers didn't like him either, as he openly stated he was smarter than they were, which obviously was not the case.

Frankie had butted heads with Walt a month earlier when he'd tried to have Frankie written up for not coming in early, but Frankie hadn't been asked and ended up getting paid on a grievance.

Although Walt had let it go, Frankie hadn't forgotten that Walt had tried to have him written up without even checking into the facts or asking.

In Frankie's mind, he owed Walt one, and now was as good a time as any to pay him back.

"Have you seen Walt yet?" Shef asked Frankie as he walked into the department.

"I saw his new ride," Frankie said. "At least I assume that pearly white ladybike is his."

"You have to see his getup. He leaves at 7:30 am. Meet me at the picnic table by the gate," Shef said as he left.

Frankie started his machines, did his checks, grabbed a coffee, and headed outside.

"The guys on third have been talking about him all night. They said he looks like a cross between a panda and a skunk," Shef giggled.

Before Frankie could comment, the front doors of the plant flew open, and Walt King came striding out in a suit of white leather.

Frankie rubbed his eyes as if he'd woke up in the Land of Oz.

DID YOU GET ONE OF THESE YET TODAY?

Shef's description had been disturbingly accurate.

The white leather coat, chaps, and do-rag were an exact color match for Walt's motorcycle, while the black helmet, goggles, gloves, and boots added a sort of "bumbling villain" touch.

"Yup. Skunk Panda nails it," Frankie said under his breath as he marveled at the ridiculous getup.

Walt's freshly waxed handlebar mustache stood ready to cut the wind as he threw a leg over the big machine, fired it up, and rode off into the morning mist.

Shef came in early the next morning and stopped to talk to Walt.

"It's a beautiful motorcycle, but it sucks that it has an oil leak already," Shef said. "Do you have an appointment to have it looked at?"

"What are you talking about?" Walt growled, as he whirled around to face Shef.

"Bill said he saw a leak where you were parked yesterday, and I saw it just now when I walked past on my way into the plant."

Walt rushed out of the department and headed to the front of the plant.

He punched out the turnstile, walked to his bike, and put his hands on his head.

"I'm going straight to the dealership when I leave the plant. I'll be standing in front of their door when they open," he informed Shef.

When Shef saw Walt the following night, he asked how the trip to the dealership went.

"It's an okay place to buy clothes, but I'm not too sure about their service department."

"At first, they tried to convince me that nothing was wrong, but then I heard the tech say a bolt on the casing might have been loose, so he'd tightened it up," Walt stated.

"I think the manager was trying to make it look like nothing was leaking, but I know what I saw," he said as he shook his head.

When the bike didn't leak for a few days, Walt thought the problem was taken care of.

But on the fourth morning, a big puddle of oil had appeared in the usual spot when Walt finished his shift.

He didn't have time to go to the dealership that day, but he did call and set up an appointment for the following morning.

"It's odd that it never leaks in my garage," Walt mumbled.

"I've heard the temperature drop outside at night has a lot to do with it," Shef offered. "It has something to do with different metals expanding and contracting at different rates, so the seals give out."

"I've also heard they have a lot of oil leak problems with the first year of any new model," he added. "It's almost like it takes them a few tries to get everything to fit together right."

"I'm going to demand they split the cases and fix it right this time," Walt told Shef.

"I spent a ton of money there, and they won't get away with taking my cash and selling me a bike that leaks."

"Well, let me know what happens on Tuesday," Shef said. "The wife and I are leaving in a few hours for a long weekend. Good luck!"

When Walt walked out that day, someone had set a coffee can under the corner of his bike where the oil spot always appeared.

The bottom of the can was coated with oil.

He shook his head and tossed the can against the fence.

Just before he pulled out, he looked up and saw someone had added the word "Leaky" above the words "Motorcycle Parking" on the sign that marked his preferred spot.

"Somebody's messing with you," the service technician told Walt.

"Don't try to convince me my motorcycle isn't leaking oil," Walt threatened. "I'm not dumb."

"How much oil have you added to the tank?" the young man challenged.

"None. But didn't you add some last time I was here?" Walt accused.

"Nope. Not a drop. It was full. Topped right off like it is right now."

"But don't the new model years always leak?" Walt protested.

"This engine design is the oldest combination we have. It never leaks. Who told you it was a new model year?" the service tech squinted.

"And no, bikes don't leak more when you park them outside at night," he added. "Don't you realize how ridiculous that sounds?"

Walt looked at the bike skeptically.

"Are you sure there's no other place to put oil in that it could be leaking out of?"

"Absolutely one hundred percent sure. That's the only place to put oil in the lower end."

Walt thought about the size of the puddles he'd seen under his bike.

There's no way his tank would still be full after leaking that much oil.

Plus, it hadn't leaked in his garage.

The technician had to be right.

Someone was playing tricks on him.

Was it Shef? It almost had to be!

He'd told Walt about the first leak, the new model year theory, and he'd proposed the idea of temperature leaks.

"I'll bet it doesn't happen while he's gone this weekend," he thought.

DID YOU GET ONE OF THESE YET TODAY?

That night when Walt came to work, the sign was amended to "Leaky High Horse Parking," so he parked two spots down.

When he got to his office, there was a Pringles can in the middle of his desk with paper taped around it that said "Leaky Harley Cleanup Kit" in marker on the side.

He could see it was full of kitty litter through the clear plastic top.

A paint brush and miniature dustpan were displayed next to it.

To the left sat a paper that said "Official Environmental Notice" that showed a map of the parking lot, a description of the leaky piece of equipment, and the threat of a fine.

Walt growled as he balled up the paper and threw it away.

"Well, it can't be Shef," Walt thought. "But who?"

He snatched the Pringles can as he turned to walk out the door, but the bottom had been cut out and it was more than half filled with ball bearings from the assembly line.

He moaned as round metal balls went bouncing across the floor, while a mushroom cloud of kitty litter dust erupted in the middle of his desk.

He ran straight to security, where he demanded to see the parking lot footage from the last three days.

When they told him the camera was broke and hadn't been recording, he hung his head and walked back to his desk.

In the end, Walt told everyone he'd hired an investigator to catch the culprit, so Frankie stopped dumping oil.

By that time, the joke had run its course, anyhow.

Although the lubricating of the asphalt stopped that day, Walt's coworkers didn't stop messing with him about his Leaky High Horse and calling him "Slick" or "Spot" when they wanted to push his buttons.

Rumor had it his pearly white trike really did develop an oil leak at some point.

But nobody really knows for sure.

THE GLITTER BOMB

"Is that...? Is that glitter on your shoulder?" Brad Porter asked.

Biff Buffman's head whipped around and cocked to the side as he eyed the sparkly flakes buried deep in the threads of his sweater.

"Why are you wearing glitter? I don't understand..." Brad teased.

"You're not married and don't have any kids. Why are you wearing glitter?" he repeated.

Biff ignored him and walked to the other side of the huddle.

Tim Shefler spotted the glitter instantly.

"You look like a princess," he beamed.

By this time, Biff had enough of their ribbing.

He turned to Brad and said loudly," The glitter came from my niece. I picked her up from a birthday party and took her home to my sister. She came out of the party covered in the stuff."

Brad and Shef both smiled but didn't say anything more.

After the meeting, the plant secretary turned to Biff and said, "I feel your pain. Glitter really sucks to clean up. I'm glad my daughters outgrew that quickly."

"I HATE GLITTER!" he complained. "I've vacuumed my truck three times since then, and there's still glitter everywhere, I'm going to have to sell it."

Brad winked at Shef as they exited the room.

Knowing what someone didn't like made it easy to mess with them.

A few days later, Tim Shefler leaned on the secretary's desk and asked if Biff was in the quality meeting.

She said he was, and he continued to make small talk as Brad Porter slipped past and walked down the hallway to Biff's office.

Brad owned a locksmith business on the outside, and he was in Biff's office in a matter of seconds.

While Tim played lookout, Brad went to work setting the trap in the top drawer of Biff's desk using a rubber band, plastic spoon, and a tube of glitter.

When the drawer was opened, the tensioned spoon would catapult glitter straight in Biff's face.

73

Brad had spent hours testing and perfecting the contraption on an old desk in an abandoned office using shredded paper instead of glitter.

Before he slid the drawer shut, he took all the pencils and pens off Biff's desk and put them in the drawer.

Once the trap was set, he put a line of glitter above the door jamb and dumped a little in the front vent of the air conditioner above Biff's desk for good measure.

Then he locked the door and quietly left.

Biff came out of his meeting and hurried down the hall to take care of a few calls before the safety walk.

He pushed the speaker button on his phone and dialed his voicemail.

He grabbed his note pad and searched for the pen that was usually there.

When he didn't find it, he leaned forward and yanked the top drawer.

He jumped at the mousetrap-like snap, then jumped again as the spoon flipped out and hit him in the top of the belly.

"Aargh!" he squeaked, as glitter bounced off his freckled cheeks and flew in his hair.

He closed his eyes, fell backwards in his chair, and waved his hands in front of his face as if he were swatting a swarm of gnats.

Biff was about ten minutes late for the safety walk that day.

DID YOU GET ONE OF THESE YET TODAY?

When he caught up to the rest of the group, he looked a little worse for the wear.

He'd stripped off his sweater, tried rinsing the glitter out of his hair in the bird bath in the management locker room, and had taken his button-up shirt off to shake it out.

He'd put himself back together in haste, and the team had never seen him in this condition.

"Wow! What happened to you?" the secretary asked

"It's been a rough day," he said, scanning the others in the group.

"Did anyone go into my office today?" he asked.

"No, and I was there the whole day. I even came in early to get ready for these meetings."

She stopped and turned to look at him.

"Is that glitter on the side of your face? Oh, and there's some in your hair!"

"Did your niece go to another party?" she asked.

"Your truck must be a mess!" she exclaimed.

Brad and Shef started laughing when they saw Biff's bling and wasted no time taking turns calling him "Princess" and "Tinkerbell".

And for the next six months, the glitter above Biff Buffman's doorjamb and in his air conditioner helped to keep those nicknames alive.

FLUSHING OUT A BIRD DOG

"We're being watched," Brad Porter said.

"I know," Charlie Sagebrush replied. "He was there about twenty minutes ago, too."

"Let's go to the crib and get those parts we need," Brad winked.

Trent Becker hunkered behind the big scrap hopper and checked his watch as the pair got on their flatbed cart and drove away.

The young boss was fresh out of college and ready to leave his mark on the world of automotive manufacturing.

In his first eight months as line-side supervisor, the 26-year-old engineering student had written over a dozen people up for various reasons.

If they stepped out of line one time, he had them.

Although he'd whipped his production crew into shape, he hadn't been able to get maintenance to respond to "line down" calls as quickly as he thought they should.

He'd gone over his boss's head a few times to complain, and he'd even told the plant manager, "Things would be different if I were in charge of maintenance."

Not long after that, Trent Becker got his chance to shine as a maintenance supervisor.

He'd soon discover it wasn't as easy to manage trades as it had been production.

DID YOU GET ONE OF THESE YET TODAY?

While production jobs are made up of timed, repetitive tasks in a controlled environment, skilled trades jobs aren't as easy to understand or assess.

It's not as bad if you have a background in trades or you have another member of management with experience to assist you, but Trent Becker had neither.

He'd spent so much time running maintenance down while he was on production that the other supervisors all hated him.

He started off slow the first week, roaming from job to job, claiming he was trying to learn what everyone was doing.

The trades didn't talk to him much because of his reputation for writing people up.

By the second week, they'd made a pact to drop their tools on the floor where they stood as soon as they saw him on their job and go talk his ear off about anything but the job.

If he tried hanging back to observe from a distance, they'd stop what they were doing and walk his way, shouting: "Can I help you?" or "Did you need me?"

Some people took a more confrontational approach, asking him to his face why he kept bird dogging them.

One guy even froze in the "dog on point" position every time he spied the young boss checking up on him.

Trent had left Charlie and Brad alone for the first few weeks because their area was so dirty and loud, but now he was out to make sure these guys weren't screwing off.

He hunkered next to the scrap hopper as they drove back in.

"Still there," Brad told Charlie out of the corner of his mouth.

Trent was standing next to their cart when they came back out from carrying parts behind the machine they were rebuilding.

"I've been here three times in the last half hour, and you guys haven't been on the job at all," he scolded.

"That's funny. You watched us leave to get parts twenty minutes ago," Sagebrush replied, as he looked at his watch. "You were standing right there in the same spot you were when we came back."

Trent looked over at his spot by the scrap hopper.

He'd have to find a better spot.

"Make sure you're here when you're on the clock until these are done," Trent ordered. "And can you guys go a little faster? There are a lot of machines that need fixing."

Trent walked away and the pair went back to work without saying a word.

After lunch, Brad elbowed Charlie in the ribs.

"Hey, do you see where that little pipsqueak is now?" he said in a low voice.

Charlie peeked around the edge of the machine and spotted Trent underneath the platform on the big filter system that sat in the middle of the room.

"It has to be filthy under there! He must have gotten all dirty getting in there," Charlie figured.

They worked a while longer until they saw Trent had left, then they walked over to where he'd been hiding.

Charlie eyed the platform that shrouded the small, dirty space Trent had crawled into.

The grating overhead was part of a raised walkway that bridged the operator platform and the filter system.

The metal dust in the area caused such a fire hazard that there were at least thirty sprinkler heads positioned all around the filter system and underneath the platform.

Sagebrush walked up the steps, and dust, rust, and soot rained from the steel steps under his heavy footfalls.

Convinced he'd seen what he needed to see, he went back to work.

During last break of the day, he went to talk with one of the pipefitters who came in early from the afternoon shift.

Charlie needed a favor, and he knew just the right guy to ask.

Just before break the next morning, Brad spotted Trent hiding in his hole.

"Now," he nodded.

Charlie ducked behind the machine he was working on and plugged two cords together.

A scream came from under the platform as water erupted from the open one-inch valve directly over Trent's head, washing thirty years' worth of dust, rust, and soot down on top of him.

He slipped and fell twice trying to get out and ended up with a mouthful of rusty mud that slid off the catwalk just as he looked up.

By the time he made it out the door, he was literally black from head to toe.

"I'm writing them both up," Trent told Jack Lang later that day after he'd gone home and cleaned up.

"Writing them up? What the hell for? You're the one who should be written up!" the old superintendent growled.

Trent cocked his head to the side.

"They pretty much saved the plant after you knocked that sprinkler head off. What were you thinking going under there?" Jack demanded.

"Wait, I never..." Trent stammered.

"The pipefitters went out and replaced the broken sprinkler head, but it was the millwrights who shut the valve off so the whole area didn't flood," Jack nodded.

"They acted quickly and saved your ass! I think you should give them an award," he finished.

Trent walked back out to their area after the meeting.

He looked under the platform and saw the sprinkler head in the middle had indeed been replaced.

But he wasn't completely stupid.

Trent knew that a sprinkler head hadn't washed all that grime down on him.

That's not where the water had been coming from.

As he could clearly see by looking at the platform above, the water had been coming from above that point, but he couldn't identify the source.

After a long time, he shook his head and accepted defeat.

It wouldn't be much longer before Trent Becker was demoted to a third shift assembly line in another plant.

FUELING UP FOR A MEETING

"Man, this room stinks!" I said to my coworker as we entered the little room where we met with our boss first thing every day.

The room did stink. It was ripe like old garbage, but also smelled like sewer.

I opened both doors to the aisle and turned the big fan on.

"It's the electricians," Jimmy said.

"Do the third shift electricians meet in here?" I asked.

"Nope. It's from the day shift guys yesterday. They have a meeting here every Wednesday at 1 pm," he added. "And man, do they EVER stink!"

"They do it because Bob Dumas makes them come to his meetings here, and they hate him and his little room," Jimmy continued.

"At first, they met in the upstairs cafeteria, but they all sat in the back and refused to participate. When he moved it here, they're trapped around this little table with him, so they changed their tactics."

"Why would a general foreman meet with the electricians every week?" I asked.

"He used to be an electrician on the floor, so it's easy for him to micromanage them. He doesn't meet with any other group of trades on a weekly basis. Just them."

"Wait, you mean they're stinking up the room on purpose?" I asked. "How are they doing that? Is there garbage hidden here somewhere? Why do we have to suffer too?"

"No, silly. They're eating food that makes them gassy. Paying him back in methane," Jimmy laughed.

I shook my head in denial.

I'd heard of 'hangtime', but this was too much to believe.

"If you don't believe me, head up to the old upstairs cafeteria next Wednesday at lunch time. You'll see."

I looked around the little room, but still didn't believe him.

There had to be something nasty hidden in here.

The hallway-shaped room was barely big enough to fit the conference table and nine metal chairs.

A shelf full of maintenance manuals lined one wall, and the other wall was windows that faced the main aisle.

DID YOU GET ONE OF THESE YET TODAY?

There really wasn't anywhere to hide garbage, but I couldn't grasp how any stench could still be this powerful after sixteen hours.

I'd have to see for myself.

The following Wednesday, I climbed the stairs that led to the old cafeteria.

A new cafeteria had been built and opened on the main floor of the plant, but it was just being brought online, so this room was still open.

When I walked in, the only people in the big room were the electricians.

(I found out later that most people had chosen to leave the old cafeteria about the same time the electricians put their stinky plan into action.)

My nose started to burn as I closed the distance across the room.

A small buffet was set up on a long table along the wall, and crock pots and hot plates were plugged in at both ends.

"Hey Kid! Have some lunch!" Craig Wonch called.

"What are you guys having?" I asked as I scrunched up my face.

They started laughing, and Billy Perow put his hand around my shoulder to guide me along their buffet.

My eyes watered as we approached the big crock pot at the end.

I lifted the lid, and the pungent odor of sauerkraut and polish sausage tickled my nose hairs.

I set it back down and saw a jar that reminded me of biology class. "What's in that?" I asked.

"Pickled pig's feet," Billy answered.

"And that one?"

"Pickled red hots."

Billy picked up a third jar, twisted off the lid, and stuck it in my face.

"DEAR GOD, WHAT THE HECK IS THAT?!??!" I gasped.

"Kimchi," Billy laughed. "It's fish-head soup. There's a little Vietnamese deli downtown that sells it."

"That's the nastiest thing I've ever smelled in my life!" I exclaimed.

"Wait a couple hours," said a voice from across the room.

Billy laughed at my reaction and pointed to a pile of Limburger cheese.

"That stuff is a close second, but I agree. Kimchi smells the worst."

Next was a big tray of deviled eggs, a smaller tray of bacon-wrapped water chestnuts, and some ham rolls with cream cheese, pickles, and onions.

It occurred to me that there were only eight guys here and enough food to feed 30 or 40.

A huge tray of vegetables sat behind the deviled eggs.

Carrot sticks, broccoli, cauliflower, peppers, and kohlrabi were piled high.

"That's to make sure there's enough fiber to get everything going," Billy smirked.

"Oh my gosh! You guys have this down to a science," I gasped.

"We've been fine-tuning for five weeks now. Like most things, it's trial and error."

"Craig shit his pants in the meeting last week," he said, matter-of-factly. "He thinks it was the cabbage soup that got him."

"Yeah," Craig admitted. "It was worth it though. Dumbass Dumas ran out of the room and puked in a trash can," he laughed.

"That's the reason I'm here," I said. I picked up your scent trail the next morning and started asking around.

I lifted the lid of another crock pot and smelled the delicious aroma of white bean and chicken soup with huge bacon chunks.

"That's the best bean soup you'll ever eat," exclaimed Billy, as he shoved a foam bowl and plastic spoon into my hands.

And he was right.

As I moved past the rest of the items on the table, I saw a bowl of caramel squares, hot chocolate, orange juice, and other miscellaneous sweets.

These guys were serious about their mission.

As I sat to eat my bean soup, they took turns telling horror stories about their weekly gas attack.

Craig really had shit his pants. He said he'd planned to dial things back a little this week, but the bean soup and deviled eggs were hard to turn down.

Billy had overdone it on the kimchi two weeks ago and ended up with diarrhea for three days.

The other guys were still trying to achieve their maximum potential.

"It took us a while to talk Jimmy into getting in on the action. He's got IBS," Billy grinned.

"Turns out it really works to his advantage," Craig added.

"Well, it's nice to see you all pulling together for a common cause," I teased.

But that was exactly what was happening.

What had started out as total disdain for a boss who micromanaged and belittled them had turned into a camaraderie of rank proportions.

Just as I finished my bowl of bean soup, the fireworks started to fly.

"Whoa, Billy. Don't waste those. Save 'em for later," coached Craig.

I got out of there quickly, but I always knew I'd tell their story one day.

It wasn't long before Bob Dumas decided to quit meeting with the electricians.

After that, the Wednesday buffets fizzled, then ended with one last ugly hurrah the day the old cafeteria was finally closed.

But that's a different story for a different book on a different day.

MR. TWINKLE TOES

"Isn't that the most ridiculous thing you've ever seen?" Frankie Ford giggled.

Tim Shefler nodded his head and laughed.

After nearly 30 years in the auto industry, neither had witnessed anything quite like this.

"SAFE-TY! QUA-LI-TY!! THROUGH-PUT!!!" the management team chanted in unison.

"I think they're going to start dancing and hugging," Frankie said. "That will help us build more cars."

"This is just as crazy as you said it was," Shef mused. "He's only been here a month! Look at them clapping and chanting and carrying on!"

"He makes them do it at the end of every meeting," Frankie added.

"Look how much they hate it," Shef snickered. "I'm teasing Buffy about this later!"

Shef was right. Not one of them liked it.

The managers, engineers, and support staff had despised the practice of chanting the plant metrics over and over since the first day he'd made them do it.

"You can do better than that!" Brant Norgan shouted. "C'mon! Louder!"

The little red sweater vest hugged his button-up a little too snugly, causing them both to ride up his slender five-foot four-inch frame every time he yelled.

His bleach-blond spike and copper-tone skin wafted a West Coast "better than you" air to everyone who called this dinosaur of a factory their home.

Brant Norgan had spent the last three years in a high-tech California factory that was a joint venture with a Japanese automaker.

He'd returned and was assigned to the plant manager role with the goal of implementing "just-in-time" manufacturing and management methods.

But it wasn't just the silly new way of doing business that upset those around him.

Brant Norgan took little man syndrome to a whole new level.

The way he yelled at his underlings was an embarrassment to everyone within earshot.

Instead of chewing people out behind a closed office door, Norgan would berate, belittle, and disrespect his subordinates in front of others, attacking their character, skills, and anything else he could think of to insult them.

DID YOU GET ONE OF THESE YET TODAY?

At his second staff meeting, he'd spent nearly five minutes screaming at a new engineer for not knowing off-hand how many parts a "critical" machine could produce per hour.

Since then, he'd left a trail of ripped asses wherever he went.

It was no wonder the staff had all started chanting and clapping from the beginning.

He had them all terrified.

Frankie took one more look at his plant's "world-class" leadership.

Clap! Clap! CLAP-CLAP-CLAP!!

"Ugh," he said, as he shook his head and walked away.

The next day, Biff Buffman and Jack Lang were headed to the morning meeting when Tim Shefler stopped them.

"Do you hear that noise? I think the bearings might be going out of that roof fan," Shef said, as he pointed up into the dark building steel.

Both superintendents looked up and strained their eyes and ears.

Shef knew, of course, that they couldn't possibly hear anything over the pounding of the presses, but he asked again anyhow.

"Did you hear me? Can you hear that?"

"I heard you. And yes, definitely a bad bearing. I'll let maintenance know," Jack Lang said, as they continued toward their meeting.

"Thanks," Shef said, admiring the new yellow paint job on the heels of their shoes as they walked away.

"Nice work!" Shef nodded, as Frankie Ford stepped out from behind the broom closet that stood next to the aisle.

"Norgan's going to lose his mind when he sees that!" Frankie said, as he wiped up the overspray with a rag he'd dipped in mineral spirits.

The new plant manager had heard rumors of people getting their heels painted, and he'd let the union know that if anyone was caught painting heels, they'd be fired on the spot.

Now his two underlings were headed straight to his Friday morning pow-wow sporting a fresh new coat of safety yellow.

Frankie and Shef slipped down the back aisle, cut through the tool crib, and stood alongside the dunnage across from the meeting area.

About twenty people were standing around making small talk when Biff and Jack reached the group.

About the same time one of the floor supervisors pulled Jack aside to tell him about his heels, Brant Norgan came out of the front office with his secretary in-tow.

When he heard people laughing, he immediately wanted to know what was funny.

When he saw Biff and Jack's heels, his face turned five shades of red.

"HOW COULD YOU BE SO STUPID??!" he screamed.

"They painted BOTH of your heels while you were wearing your shoes!? What, were you sleeping?"

"How can I trust you to manage this plant when you can't even pay attention to what's going on right under your goddamned feet?" he insulted.

He started to turn away, but whirled around sarcastically and said, "Or did you dummies paint each other's heels? Was that it?"

"Go clean yourselves up!"

About an hour after the meeting, a memo showed up on the break table stating that the plant manager had notified the union that anyone caught painting anyone's heels will be fired on the spot.

"In addition, all paint must now be requisitioned from the main crib, as the point of use paint cabinets are being eliminated."

Frankie noticed the memo was not signed or stamped by the union.

They'd never agree to anything so silly.

About 10:30 am, a small group of people showed up in Frankie's department to run through a new method of gaging parts.

This system had been developed by the Japanese and was being driven by Brant Norgan, who would be performing the demonstration himself at the afternoon quality walk.

Frankie watched from across the department as Norgan ran through the 11-step gaging process.

His huddled minions winced in perfect time with his jerky motions, nodding and cowering with clipboards clamped tight to their chests like backwards turtle shells.

He finished the last step, placed the part back in the custom foam holder, and touched the tips of his fingers together as if he'd just finished conducting an orchestra.

Then he kick-turned to face the group, nodded, and dismissed them.

About quarter to one, the group of engineers, managers, union representatives, and other members who made up the plant quality council gathered in front of the long gage table to watch Norgan demonstrate the new process.

After a brief introduction by Jack Lang, Brant Norgan stepped to the gage table to do his thing.

He ran through the first few gages just fine, but the fourth gage was missing.

There was an outline where the gage should have been, but it wasn't there.

He looked up and saw the edge of the gage sticking out from the shelf above, so he set the part down and reached up to grab it.

It was quite a stretch, but he got it to start sliding off the ledge after a couple good tugs.

At that exact moment, two puffs of pink paint billowed from underneath the table and dissipated as the plant manager finished wrestling the heavy gage down off the shelf.

A few gasps could be heard as Norgan finished checking the part, but nobody said a word.

He sniffed a couple of times as he touched his fingers together like he'd practiced.

But his kick-turn got ugly as the wet paint caused his left shoe to slide out from underneath him and sent him flying backwards into the big table.

"What th…"

That's all he got out before he righted himself and followed the group's wide-eyed gaze straight down to his feet.

His jaw dropped open, and his eyes bulged in disbelief.

Big globs of bright pink paint dripped off both sides of his shiny black shoes.

His argyle socks were covered in front, and the cuffs of his pant legs wore a respectable first coat.

He spun and ran to the back of the gage table, nearly wiping out as he rounded the corner, but there was nobody to be found.

"WHO DID IT?!!?" he screamed at the group, as he flew back around front.

"I KNOW YOU SAW WHO DID IT!"

"We didn't notice your shoes until you turned around," lied Biff Buffman.

"He must have done it when you reached up to move that gage down," added Jack Lang. "I think you should keep that gage down in the row with the others."

Norgan clenched his teeth, shook his fist, and stormed off toward his office.

He'd had enough for the week.

Next week he'd find out who did this and make them pay.

By Monday morning, the whole plant knew it was either Frankie Ford or Tim Shefler who had painted the plant manager's shoes.

On Tuesday afternoon, one of the engineering tattletales told Norgan that - according to the rumor mill - it was either Frankie or Shef.

Since this was Biff Buffman's area of the plant, Norgan grabbed him and headed to confront these two sleazy vandals.

"Well, if it isn't Mr. Twinkletoes," Frankie jabbed as Norgan came storming up.

The committeeman had let Frankie know Norgan was heading his way.

"I COULD FIRE YOU RIGHT NOW, FORD!" the angry little man screamed.

"I was here before you got here, and I'll be here after you're gone," Frankie said calmly.

"THEY SAID IT WAS YOU!" Norgan hissed, as he pointed at Frankie's chest.

DID YOU GET ONE OF THESE YET TODAY?

Frankie had never been this close to Norgan, and it made him happy to realize he was at least two inches taller than this pipsqueak.

"Who said it was me?" Frankie grinned. "Nobody saw me do it, and even the ones who did will still say it wasn't me!"

A vein bulged out of Norgan's forehead, pushing his glasses down his nose as the bows pulled his ears out to the side.

"Even your own people..." Frankie's voice trailed off as he pursed his lips and clucked his tongue.

By this time, a few others had stumbled upon the little gathering but soon found themselves staring at the floor wishing they were somewhere else as Norgan blew up.

"I'LL HAVE YOUR JOB!!!" he screamed.

"Then either fire me or drag your ass," Frankie stated flatly, gesturing behind him with his thumb over his shoulder.

"I...I DON'T HAVE TO LEAVE! I RUN THIS PLANT!!" Norgan bellowed.

"I guess you're right. You ARE the plant manager," Frankie shrugged.

"But, if you do decide to leave, there's one more thing you should know before you go."

All eyes were on Frankie as he slowly raised his hands and said:

"You're the only plant manager I ever met who has to jump up and wave his arms to flush the urinal."

And he started laughing, waving his arms, and wiggling his hips as he bounced up and down.

Norgan tried to ignore Frankie's antics but lost his cool when his managers couldn't stop themselves from cracking up.

The nickname Twinkletoes followed him to his next assignment, where he was later terminated for harassment.

Chapter Four

Fighting Like Brothers and Sisters

FARM GIRL VS BIKER LADY

The best "catfight" I ever saw wasn't in a ring, in a bar, or on a television or movie screen.

By far, the hardest-hitting girl-on-girl action I ever witnessed happened just after lunch on an assembly line in a busy automotive factory.

BRANDY BOOTH

Sammy Stevens was an "old lady" as biker lingo goes.

The forty-six-year-old was the wife of a high-ranking member of a notorious motorcycle club, and she was well-known for not taking lip from anyone.

Sammy was relatively tall, maybe 5'-10", with brunette hair-dyed red and a wiry build.

Becky Johnson was the typical farm-girl type in her mid-twenties. She'd been the softball star in high school who married the football star and had their first baby about a year ago.

She stood 5'-5" with thick thighs, a wide ponytail, and a body that looked like she was good at throwing hay bales.

From what I learned afterward, these two hadn't liked one another for quite some time.

While it's easy to understand how anger can build up, nobody could have predicted what would happen on this day.

I was driving my weld buggy past the assembly area when a plastic parts bin came flying out into the aisle and bounced into the next department.

I expected to see some guy had thrown the dunnage to mess with me, but to my surprise, I looked over at the line and saw fists and hair flying.

I jerked my cart to the side of the aisle just in time to see the coordinator pull the emergency stop cord above the assembly line.

DID YOU GET ONE OF THESE YET TODAY?

As I rolled to a stop, a tall point of use rack holding tags, paint pens, and gloves tipped over and exploded as it hit the floor.

I had to see who was causing all this commotion.

When I ran across the aisle into the department, Becky Johnson was completely airborne from being swung around by her ponytail and hoodie.

Sammy let go of both, throwing Becky sideways into a row of lockers that – luckily – was bolted to the floor.

"So, you wanna pull hair, huh?" Becky screamed, as her powerful thighs drove her up from the floor and straight into Sammy's chest.

Sammy didn't expect her to come up that quickly, and the force of Becky's attack almost flipped her backwards over the assembly line.

Becky wasted no time in pulling her back upright - by her hair.

Gobs of red hair stuck between her fingers as her fist crashed into side of the old biker's face three or four times.

Somehow, Sammy ended up with a rubber mallet in her hand, which Becky immediately grabbed with both hands and threw to the floor.

She took a couple steps back and grabbed the round garbage can marked "Dirty Gloves" and raised it high above her head.

Sammy ducked down as Becky slammed the plastic barrel on top of her, but it bounced off the side of the line and split down the side.

Sammy shoved it to the side and grabbed the front of Becky's sweatshirt and used it to pull her down in front of the line.

Becky let out a scream as Sammy grabbed one of the hanging air ratchets and brought it down hard on top of her head.

The coordinator jumped in to stop it at this point, but the blow took a lot out of Becky and Sammy was clearly going to win.

Both girls were sent out the door for two weeks and relocated to different plants upon their return.

WANNA BITE?

"Apprentices are lower than whale shit at the bottom of the ocean," Larry Lambert told Skip Heinrich the day they'd met.

"You ever get dog shit on the bottom of your shoe?" he continued.

"Sucks, doesn't it? But you're way lower than that. You're whale-shit low. Even lower."

Skip ignored the banter and shook the next tradesman's hand.

He'd need to have thick skin if he was going to make it in this plant.

Larry was the second guy who had tried to ride him in his first hour here.

The first guy called himself the Pope and had "blessed" the new apprentices by putting a white filter on his head and spritzing them with water from a spray bottle that had a cross drawn on it.

DID YOU GET ONE OF THESE YET TODAY?

Now he was standing in front of this clown.

"Remember, boy," Larry said as he pointed down. "Whale shit."

"Well, I guess there's only one way for me to go from here," Skip answered, with a half-hearted thumbs-up and a wink.

It didn't take long for Skip to realize that Larry thought it was cool to mistreat apprentices.

He'd called Andy Carrier stupid for being slow and careful while running the crane they were using to set a big motor on a broach machine.

Andy had gotten flustered and walked off the job, so Skip had to work with Larry to finish installing the motor.

"I hope you're a better operator than that other dumb apprentice," Larry poked.

But Skip just focused on the job and wrapped it up quickly.

"I can't stand the guy," Andy complained to Skip. "He's mean all the time. It's like he's miserable and can't be happy unless everyone else is miserable too."

"He told me I have to come to work early every day to get my tools on the fork truck he likes to drive so nobody else takes it."

"He also told me to have him a coffee ready, but I'm not getting him coffee every day. I have to draw the line somewhere," Andy shook his head.

Skip had been lucky the first two months at this plant. He'd only had to work with Larry the one time, but he knew his turn was coming.

Andy was reaching his breaking point.

"You know what he did to me the other day when we were all standing around our boxes before break?" Andy asked.

"He pulled a candy bar out of his pocket, took a bite, and shoved it in my face, saying 'Wanna bite'? I tried to turn away, but he chased me around with it. He's just an old bully," Andy whined.

It didn't take long after that before Skip was assigned to work with Larry.

Andy had gone to the union and told them he was going to wrap a pipe around Larry's head, and the committeeman had informed the boss that it might be time for a change.

Skip didn't have any problems with Larry at first.

When it came down to it, Larry was a top-notch skilled tradesman.

He was a sculptor with a cutting torch and the best fabricator in the shop.

But this still didn't give him the right to treat others as badly as he did.

Skip let Larry know right away that he wasn't going to get him coffee every morning.

"I don't drink coffee," Skip explained. "I'd just make the people at the coffeepot mad for not knowing coffeepot etiquette."

This didn't please Larry, but he let it slide.

"But I will do my best to get the fork truck you like. I agree, it's the best truck in the plant," Skip assured Larry.

Things went smoothly for the first week they worked together.

Skip was a farm kid who had done well in metal shop, so he was already a decent fabricator.

On Monday the following week, Skip went to get their fork truck and it was already being used by other millwrights who had been assigned to move warehouse material.

"What are we going to do now, dumbass?" Larry wanted to know. "If you'd gotten here earlier, we'd have our truck."

Skip looked down and took a breath.

"Brad says he only needs it for a couple hours this morning, then he'll give it back to us. I figured we could fab up a few more pieces in the shop and take it all out when we get our truck back."

When Skip looked up, Larry's face was beet red.

"And who made YOU the goddamned journeyman?" he exploded.

"You're too stupid to even get our fork truck, let alone plan what to do on a job!"

Skip could see he wasn't going to reason his way out of this.

He'd have to figure something else out – and quick.

"Look, I screwed up," he apologized. "I'll tell you what. I'll buy your pop and candy bar at break to make it up to you."

This seemed to catch Larry off guard, and he backed off a little.

"I suppose we have more we can do in the shop," Larry said.

They worked a couple hours and headed to break.

Everyone in a factory has their favorite go-to out of the vending machines.

Some like Mountain Dew and Cheetos, some like Pop Tarts and milk.

Larry Lambert's favorite combination was a Payday candy bar and a Coca Cola Classic.

Every day about a quarter to nine, he'd buy the same two things from the vending machines next to the skilled trades break area.

He'd stick the candy bar in his pocket and set the pop on his box where the crew gathered prior to break.

As Skip handed Larry his snack that morning, he wondered if this candy bar would end up jammed in his face as Larry had done to Andy.

But Larry had calmed down a bit when Brad brought their fork truck back, and he seemed pretty quiet.

"He must be over it," Skip thought, as Larry finished his candy bar.

But Skip was dead wrong.

Larry was NOT over it.

When break was over, Skip started to get on the truck next to Larry.

"No, not you," glared Larry. "Only me. You walk to the job. Maybe then you'll get to the truck a little earlier next time."

Skip looked up at Larry and groaned.

"Don't just stand there with that dumb look on your face. You'd better start walking so you're on the job when I get there," Larry ordered, as he drove off down the aisle.

Larry made Skip walk the whole day.

He went several places he didn't need to go, stopping along the way to brag to everyone that he was making his apprentice walk for being lazy and stupid.

With about an hour to go, Skip quit following Larry and went to talk with Lisa.

He hid out the rest of the day and waited until Larry had gone home to lock up his tools.

Larry was waiting by Skip's box when he walked in the next day.

"So, you want to disappear, huh? Do it again and I'll go to the apprentice coordinator and let him deal with your sorry ass," Larry threatened.

Larry made Skip walk again that morning.

This time, he made him carry his own tool bag from job to job.

"We never used to have trucks to haul our tools when I was an apprentice," Larry sneered.

105

Skip's tool bag was too heavy to carry around, but he did it anyway.

By the time first break rolled around, Skip was ready to explode.

When he arrived at the break area seven minutes late, Larry was leaning on his box telling the others how dumb Skip was for not getting there on time.

As Skip set his tools down and tried to walk past, Larry whipped the candy bar out of his pocket, ripped the end open, and peeled the wrapper back.

"Oh, hell no," thought Skip, as he jumped to the side and ducked his head away.

Larry didn't have time to take a bite, but Skip was obviously on the run, so he stuck it in his face anyway and said loudly, "Wanna bite?"

Knowing Larry hadn't taken a bite, Skip whirled around, grabbed Larry's wrist, and bit more than half the candy bar off.

"YOU DUMB SONOFABITCH!" Larry screamed. "You... You bit me!!"

Skip raised his arms and moved back, but not too far.

Nuts rained from his mouth as he leaned in and chomped loudly in Larry's face while growling like a junk yard dog.

Larry backed up, shook his fist, spun, and stormed off down the aisle, spiking the half-eaten candy bar in the yellow trash can that sat next to his truck.

Since the maintenance leader had been standing there when the incident occurred, Skip was never assigned to work with Larry again.

For the record, only two people know for sure if Skip bit Larry that day.

Although both have been asked publicly, neither seems to want to talk about it.

STRIKE THREE, YOU'RE OUT!

Sharing isn't just a problem for preschoolers, kindergarteners, and folks under five years of age.

Sharing can also be a problem for men in their fifties and sixties who pride themselves as experts in their field and call themselves skilled tradesmen.

Yes, you heard it here first.

Sometimes grown men fight over the silliest of things.

One such fight happened over a pipe machine during the mid-nineties between a pipefitter named Elmer Smith and an electrician named Dirk Baggshaw.

Elmer was a big farmer with rosy cheeks, a huge nose, and a noticeable limp.

Dirk was a little rat-looking fellow with thin, greasy hair and eyes that darted around in a way that made everyone around him uncomfortable.

He regularly got into fights with others for violating them in some way.

Today was no different.

Electricians and pipefitters use the same machine to cut and thread pipe, but they have to change out the dies depending on if they're threading pipe or electrical conduit.

Most of the time, other trades ask the person using the machine if they can switch it over to do their job and switch the dies back when they're done.

Dirk's approach was to wait until the person left their job, switch the dies, do his job, and walk away without cleaning up or changing the dies back.

On this particular day, Elmer Smith had taken a pipe machine out on a job and set it up to whip out some water line.

When he realized he'd forgotten his plumb bob, he jumped on his cart with his apprentice (Luke) and headed back to get one.

When they returned minutes later, Dirk had already changed out the dies and was trying to thread a three-foot piece of two-inch aluminum conduit.

"Get away from my pipe machine!" Elmer bellowed.

"You switched it over yesterday, left a mess, and never put the pipe dies back in! Go use the machine in the electrical shop!"

Elmer had good reason to be mad. He hadn't realized Dirk had changed the dies, and his pipe connections had all leaked as a result.

"I'll just be a minute," Dirk hissed, as he spun the lock to tighten the chuck onto the conduit.

"I SAID, DRAG YOUR ASS!!" Elmer screamed, as he grabbed the chuck from the other side and yanked it so the conduit came loose.

The apprentice and I looked across at each other.

This was surprising but not completely unexpected.

These two guys hated each other with a passion.

Their feud had been going on for years, but today would be a day they'd both remember.

Dirk shoved Elmer in the belly, locked the pipe back in, and stomped on the foot controller to start the machine.

Elmer grabbed the locking mechanism to keep himself from falling backward, and the pipe came free once again.

The third time Dirk tightened it, Elmer grabbed the lock and gave it a spin that would have made Bob Barker proud.

The pipe fell out with a bang and Elmer reached across the machine, grabbed Dirk by the front of his coveralls, and started to pull him into the running pipe machine.

If he didn't stop stepping on the pedal, his face would be pummeled by the spinning chuck.

About the time the chuck stopped spinning, Dirk's hand came out from inside the pipe machine gripping the three-foot piece of aluminum pipe.

Elmer didn't see it because the two were locked together on top of the machine, but the apprentice saw it and tried to knock it away before Dirk could whack Elmer upside the head.

Too late.

The aluminum pipe made a 'thud' every time it hit Elmer's head and a 'ting' when it hit the pipe machine as he pulled it back.

He connected three or four times, sending Elmer's hat and glasses flying across the department before Luke could pry the conduit free.

By the time enough people showed up to pull them apart, half the plant knew there had been a fight and both 'men' got two weeks off.

YOUR TEAM SUCKS!

"I hope all your teams get their asses kicked," poked Ritchie Robinson loudly.

The group turned to look at him but didn't say a word.

It didn't pay to egg him on.

They all knew what he would do anyhow.

Gus Briggs turned back to the others and continued, "Michigan's offense looks unstoppable lately, so we've got a pretty good chance of beating Ohio State."

"Michigan couldn't beat Ohio State if they played against their cheerleaders," Ritchie jeered. "They'd be lucky to beat a good high school team."

A few got up to go back to their jobs.

If Ritchie wasn't leaving, they were.

"And Bob, if you're dumb enough to think the Tigers can beat the Yankees in the playoffs, you're not even paying attention," Ritchie sneered.

"Nobody was even talking to you," Bob shot back angrily.

But that didn't matter to Ritchie Robinson.

It never mattered.

Ritchie was going to put his two cents in wherever he wanted, regardless of what anyone else thought.

And it didn't matter what sport they were talking about.

If Ritchie knew someone was rooting for one team, he'd cheer even louder for the other.

He did it in baseball, basketball, college and professional football, auto racing, golf, hockey, and any other competitive sport one could possibly take an interest in.

He did this regardless of the fact that he didn't know anything about sports at all.

He'd never watched them.

He'd never played them.

Truth be told, he probably didn't even know a touchdown from a home run or a bogey from a foul.

No, Ritchie Robinson wasn't into sports at all.

But he WAS into the fact that sports provided him an easy way to irritate people.

He especially liked how emotional those stupid sports fanatics would get when dreaming about their team's chances of taking home the big trophy.

This made them easy prey for a guy like Ritchie who was always out to push buttons.

And with football season in full-swing and the World Series of baseball only a few weeks away, the banter was really heating up.

As Ritchie walked back to his job, he passed a guy wearing a NASCAR hat, and it gave him an idea that made him grin from ear to ear.

It was time to add some bling to his game.

When Michigan got beat by Ohio State that Saturday, Ritchie ran out and bought an Ohio State jersey to wear to work on Monday.

When Gus spotted that bright red OSU jersey from atop his fork truck, it worked better than a bullfighter's cape.

First it enraged him.

Then it sucked him in.

"You're a real piece of work!" Gus bellowed. "What an idiot!!"

Ritchie stuck out his chest, ran up to the truck, and informed Gus that he'd have to change his wardrobe if he wanted to wear winner's clothes.

After all, Michigan hadn't beaten OSU in nearly a decade, and the next decade wasn't looking good, either.

Gus nearly hit a column as he sped away, and he glared at Ritchie from a distance the entire day.

Ritchie's outfit ended up irritating so many of his coworkers that buying the Yankees jersey was a no-brainer when the Tigers lost in game seven.

"You're just mad because your team sucks!" he'd yell at those passing by who didn't appreciate his choice of clothing.

It became so much fun that Ritchie even looked forward to going to work on the day after a big loss.

He bought jerseys, hoodies, tee shirts, hats, flags, bobble head mascots, and coffee mugs from every opposing team imaginable.

It was almost unbelievable that a guy who didn't watch sports at all had more sportswear than many true sports fans.

But as fun as the whole situation was, Ritchie still found ways to push things too far.

He'd tried the same thing with high school sports but decided against it after two angry moms threatened to plant him in a corn field.

After all, you've gotta watch those farm girls...

And not long after that, Ritchie came to work with two black eyes and a fat lip.

Apparently, he'd worn the wrong jersey to the wrong bar on the wrong night and someone wasn't in the mood for his nonsense.

After that, he only wore sportswear to work.

YOU BEEN HAD!!

"Everyone thinks I'm an asshole!" Gus Briggs wailed, as he shoved open the union office door about eight o'clock on Friday morning.

He stormed across the room and stood next to Danny Goodman's desk with his fists clenched by his side.

The senior union rep had learned to slow-play situations like these, and he paused before looking up from the report he'd been reading.

Gus's farmer pants and Michigan hoodie were tattered from his days in the factory and nights in the barnyard.

"It's okay," Danny shrugged. "Everyone thinks I'm an asshole, too."

"This isn't funny!" Gus squawked. "Ritchie has everyone in the whole plant thinking I'm an asshole. They're all honking and waving and laughing at me."

"I got so mad at the girls sorting on the corner that I finally gave them a piece of my mind!" the round farmer ranted.

"I came here because I'm about thirty seconds away from grabbing Ritchie by the neck and squeezing until I feel better," Gus seethed.

"Easy, Gus. Tell me what happened. From the start," Danny directed.

"I was waiting for Ritchie to move his stacker out of my way yesterday afternoon so I could load the stock racks next to his department."

"He was messing with me and wouldn't get out of my way, so I finally told him to move his ass, and he called me an asshole."

"Then he started saying that everyone in the plant thinks I drive like an asshole, and that he was going to have them honk and cheer because I'm such an asshole."

"And the thing is – EVERYONE'S actually doing it!"

"I don't know how he got word around so fast, but people I hardly ever see are laughing and honking at me! I can't do my job like this! You have to do something!"

Danny got up from his desk, stretched, and strolled to the office window.

"Who's gonna win the big game tomorrow, Gus?" he asked softly.

Gus exploded.

"Haven't you listened to a goddamned word I said? I need help here! I'm going to get fired if this keeps up!"

"I'm trying to help you, Gus," Danny said calmly. "Who do you want to win?"

"I can't believe you!" Gus seethed.

115

Gus looked at Danny and decided he wasn't going to be able to get him excited, so he backed off and said, "You know I'm pissed and don't want to talk football right now. And even if I did, you know I'd say Michigan is going to win tomorrow."

"I'm the biggest Michigan fan around here. Everyone knows that. Why would you ask me something so stupid?"

Because the sign on the back of your fork truck says, "Honk and wave if you want Michigan to win."

Gus turned to the window and let out a gasp.

You could almost hear the 'thud' from his jaw hitting his chest.

He stood that way a while before slowly rubbing his head and swearing under his breath.

"I've got some apologizing to do," he mumbled, as he slumped and walked out the door.

"See you later, Asshole," Danny waved. "I hope your team wins tomorrow!"

NO CLOTHES FOR YOU!

"Use your thumb to hold light pressure on the allen wrench while you tickle the tumblers from back to front until they all click into place," Brad Porter coached.

Skip pulled the pick out of the lock, thought for a second, and shoved it three quarters of the way back in.

He wiggled and pushed, and the mechanism gave way.

"I felt them all click except the third one," Skip explained. "When I went back and tickled it, it came unstuck and fell into place."

"Well, these locks are pretty old, and they may have gotten paint in the tumbler when they were spray-bombed," Brad said.

Skip looked at the locks he'd just picked.

One had been painted green and the other was bright orange.

(Paint matching is common practice for people who carry a lot of keys in the auto industry.)

"Do you need these locks for anything?" Brad asked the coordinator.

"No, they were left there when someone retired. There's no key," she said. "We think one of the old coordinators used these lockers for storage."

"What are you going to do with them?" Gus Briggs cut in.

"Probably either throw them in the scrap or let Skip practice on them," Brad replied.

"Can I have 'em?" Gus asked.

"What are you going to do with a couple old locks?" Brad wanted to know.

"Someone keeps taking the chair we use by the shipping dock and moving it down a few bays," Gus explained.

"I have a length of chain. I'll use them to lock one end around the post and one around the base of the chair. I'd never need to open them," he persuaded.

"I've got plenty of other locks to practice on," Skip said, as he handed the locks to Gus.

"Besides, these are pretty stiff and rusty," he said.

"That's perfect for what I need them for," smiled Gus.

Skip was late getting to the locker room that afternoon.

"You're going to get whistle-bit (late for leaving)," Brad had told him as he locked up his box.

Skip didn't really care. He had a couple hours to kill before class.

As the locker room emptied, he could hear someone swearing from a couple rows away, followed by loud banging.

Skip peeked around the corner and saw Ritchie Robinson standing in front of his lockers with his hands on his hips.

The only thing he had on was a small towel and the flip flops he wore in the shower.

He grabbed at the locker doors and yanked again, but they remained shut.

As Ritchie let go of the handles, Skip could see the locks – an orange one and a green one – hanging from the hasps.

"Who did this?" Ritchie screamed.

Skip ducked back around the corner and headed for his truck.

He wasn't getting caught up in this mess.

Ritchie waited for someone to come along to help, but it's not easy to talk people into helping when they're rushing the gate at the end of the shift.

It's even harder when your name is Ritchie Robinson and you've done your absolute best to insult everyone you encounter.

Nobody was interested in helping Ritchie at all.

They wouldn't even lend him a pair of dirty coveralls to wear to go get help.

In the end, Ritchie had no other choice but to walk through the cafeteria, down the stairs, down the aisle to the crib where the bolt cutters were kept, and all the way back before he could get into the lockers where his clothes were.

HONK IF YOU LIKE FUNNY THINGS!

"Get out of our office," Sam Wolzak seethed, as he pointed toward the door.

"And stop coming in here every morning," Frank Sturm growled, as he came out of the back room.

"Aww, you guys love me," Greg Flower said, as he blew them a kiss and walked out the door.

They watched as he jumped on his three-wheeled cart, zipped fifty yards down the aisle, and slammed on his brakes next to the morning huddle.

"He's getting on my nerves," Sam said, as he shook his head.

"If he thinks he's going to sit in here every day and watch for those girls to walk out so he can drive up and talk to them, he's got another thing coming," Frank replied.

For more than a week now, Greg Flower had shown up in their office at quarter to eight and made small talk while he watched for the girls up front to join the morning huddle.

Then he'd jump on his cart and rush up to talk with them until the plant manager kicked off the morning meeting.

The next morning, Greg showed up as usual.

"Hey fellas," Greg said, as he leaned to look out the window.

Neither answered as they kept reading their paper.

Greg sat down in the chair by the desk but got right back up as he noticed Becky crossing the aisle a little early.

He left without saying another word.

"That's it," said Sam.

The next morning when Greg walked in, Sam was sitting at his desk when Frank called from the back office.

"Hahaha! Holy shit, Sam! You've gotta see this!" Frank laughed.

Greg wanted to stay at his post, but he knew he had a few minutes and curiosity got the better of him.

As he went into the back room, Jimmy Labowski (the third shift electrician) knelt next to Greg's cart with a wire that had an alligator clip on both ends.

He popped back up as quickly as he'd knelt and walked away without being noticed.

After Greg had checked out what Frank thought was so funny (he didn't agree), he went back to his post to scan the aisle.

Like clockwork, the three young women emerged from the tunnel doors and walked across the aisle.

Greg jumped out of his chair, rushed out the door, and sped off on his cart.

As he approached the meeting area, the assistant plant manager and the plant superintendent came out of the tunnel to cross the aisle and join the meeting.

When Greg hit the brake, his horn blared, causing the two managers in the crosswalk to jump.

He let off the brake and the horn stopped momentarily, which seemed to confuse him and made him look down.

That brief pause was all it took.

He looked back up and realized he was no longer going to be able to stop in time for the crosswalk, so he cranked the wheel to avoid the startled bosses and hit the brakes again.

"HHOONNKK!!" the horn screamed, as the cart rocked up on two wheels.

All eyes were on Greg as his cart bounced off a post and slow-tipped onto its side, dumping the box of connectors that always rode on the back.

Nobody was injured, but Greg was a little shook up.

He stopped coming into the office after that.

Chapter Five

Overboard Paybacks

Sometimes the punishment far outweighs the crime.

MAGAZINE MADNESS

"C'mon, Kid. Help us out," Brad Porter told Skip Hendrich.

"Not the apprentice. Leave him out of this," Tim Shefler advised.

Skip looked at the pile of white paper cards on the table.

"Are those subscription cards out of magazines?" Skip asked.

Nobody said a word.

They all kept writing and throwing the finished cards into a bowl in the middle of the table.

When the bowl was filled, they dumped it into a green canvas bag that sat on a bench in the corner and started over.

Skip saw a local address written in marker on a sheet of paper taped to the wall.

"Whose address is that?" he wondered aloud.

Again, nobody said a word.

They just continued to write and repeat.

As Skip began to examine the pile of magazine inserts more closely, Shef dumped another plastic shopping bag of subscription cards on the table.

There were magazines from every topic, interest, and genre.

Hunting, fishing, snowmobiling, naked women books, naked men books, home and garden, food preservation, beekeeping, pool playing, guitar playing, rock and roll, Civil War relics, aviation, bow fishing, salsa dancing, French pastries, breastfeeding, self-defense, rock collecting, airbrushing...

You get the point.

There seemed to be ten thousand cards between all the piles.

"Where did these come from?" Skip wanted to know. "I'd never imagined there were so many different magazines."

DID YOU GET ONE OF THESE YET TODAY?

"My wife works at a dentist's office," Shef said. "And Brad's wife works at a bookstore. We've had them and a few others collecting inserts for us for over six months now."

"Buffy's gonna lose his mind," Brad giggled.

Skip looked down at the card in front of Brad and saw Biff Buffman's name above the address.

"Shef found his address on a piece of mail lying on the floor outside his office," Brad said.

"Sure he did," laughed Skip.

"Everyone's going to drop a few in different mailboxes each day until they're all gone," Shef said.

Skip shook his head, smiled, and kept walking.

This was their fight, and it was in his best interest not to get involved.

He had to laugh, though.

This little gathering was going to produce a never-ending tidal wave of magazines in Biff Buffman's mailbox for months and years to come.

Did he deserve it?

These guys all thought so.

Biff had been throwing his weight around, writing people up for trivial things and making cuts to the budget that negatively affected their paychecks while pumping up his own bonus.

Now he was about to get hit by a karma train full of blue-collar guys wielding ink pens.

"And the world goes 'round and 'round," Skip thought.

A CURE FOR PARKING IN THE AISLE

It doesn't matter where you go.

In every automotive factory in the world, there's one or two people who park in the middle of the aisle and block traffic without caring that others have a job to do.

Either they shoot the breeze with another person on a cart, fork truck, or on foot, or they park their cart in the aisle while they walk over and talk to someone off to the side.

When you say something about letting you through, they act like the whole thing is your fault, and they have more right to that space than you do.

Dirk Baggshaw was a chronic aisle-blocker.

The weasel-like electrician loved to be in everyone's way.

His coworkers would grease his steering wheel, take his key, and leave angry notes on the seat of his high flatbed.

Dirk didn't care.

The pipefitters would put his tools under his tires so he'd run them over as he drove away and he'd have to stop and pick them up.

The millwrights even lifted the back of his cart up with a fork truck and put blocks under the axles so the rear tires were barely off the ground and the cart wouldn't go.

Dirk seemed to enjoy this little game, and he continued to violate everyone else's aisle space.

After a while, his angry coworkers started to move his cart, hide it, and park it so it was wedged in between things.

They left it out behind the pond one day, hoisted it up on top of a mezzanine a different time, and even sent it to the final assembly plant a hundred miles away in the back of a semi.

Yet Dirk continued to block the aisle everywhere he went.

One day, he made the mistake of blocking the aisle too long in a guy's area who wasn't the brightest bulb on the tree.

When the guy got angry, Dirk told him where he could shove it, and then he hopped on his cart but still sat in the way.

The guy started to walk away but looked down and saw a chain lying on the floor that was still hooked on a guardrail that had just been installed.

He quietly hooked the end of the chain inside the lip of the rear bumper on Dirk's cart.

Of course, Dirk took off like a bat out of hell like he always did, and when he hit the end of that chain, the back of the cart jumped up in the air and whipped violently sideways.

He flew off the corner, did a complete front-flip, and landed on his face and hands with his boots almost touching the back of his head.

Those who saw it called the move "Somersault to Scorpion".

He was taken out in an ambulance that day, and safety had a hard time figuring out exactly what had happened.

Now, you'd think an experience like that might cause someone to change their ways, but it did not.

In the end, the only thing that would cure Dirk Baggshaw's aisle-blocking problem was retirement.

HAS ANYONE SEEN MY TOOLBOX?

Automotive factories are big places with lots of room to hide things.

When new maintenance leaders are put on from within the trades, their toolbox stays in the plant, but sits alongside their office or gets tucked away in a dusty corner.

The week before Rocky was put on as leader, he'd gotten into an argument with Rob Robeson about the right way to weld roof support steel.

Rocky was old-fashioned and wanted to do it the old way, while Rob wanted to save time and labor and take a few "harmless" shortcuts.

They ended up doing it Rocky's way, but not before Rocky had gone off on a condescending rant about how terrible Rob was at welding, rigging, and millwright-ing in general.

Rob was too mad to argue that day, but he wasn't the type to forget.

DID YOU GET ONE OF THESE YET TODAY?

About two weeks after Rocky went on as leader, Rob was given another job to weld roof support steel not far down the aisle from Rocky's office.

Rocky wouldn't be there over the weekend, but Rob's job was to build two sets of supports for new machine stacks scheduled to be installed in the coming weeks.

On Friday, Rocky tried to tell Rob how to do the job.

"I'm doing it my way. I'm a card-carrying journeyman and I'll do it any way I damn well please!" he shouted.

"I'm just saying, that's close to my office and I don't want that shit coming down on my head," Rocky griped.

"It's a hundred yards from your office," Rob shot back. "And it wouldn't hurt you if it hit you in the head anyhow. It would probably just bend the steel."

Rob did the job his own way that weekend.

He was working with Brad Porter, and Brad didn't care either way, as he was just the crane operator.

As Rob was coming down from the steel, he looked toward Rocky's office and spotted Rocky's toolbox tucked in a nook around the corner.

"Just one more pick after break," Rob told Brad.

"Oh, ok. I thought we were done," said Brad.

"One more," Rob said. "Meet me back here after break."

When Brad rounded the corner on his way back to the job, it took him a minute to believe what he could clearly see.

Directly outside Rocky's office, the crane was rigged up to Rocky's toolbox, and the Genie lift and welding machine had been moved into position.

Rob climbed in, winked, and gave Brad the thumb's up signal.

"Boom up," he directed, as Brad started laughing and hopped in the cab.

The motor grunted as the boom arm hoisted the 1,200-pound monster into the air.

"Worried about my welds letting go and dropping shit on your head, huh?" Rob mumbled under his breath as he rode alongside the box into the steel above Rocky's office.

It took some doing, but the pair positioned the toolbox high against a truss in a spot where the lights couldn't quite reach.

Rob chipped off the paint and laid four nice welds across the back of the box.

He gave Brad the "cable down" signal, unhooked the straps, and lowered himself to the ground.

As they admired their handiwork, they both agreed it couldn't be seen unless you were looking for it.

It was a matte black toolbox in a dirty corner of a dimly lit plant.

If you looked right at it and knew it was there, you could easily pick out the four red dangling wheels on aluminum casters, but it wasn't easy to see.

Because he didn't work out of his toolbox, it took Rocky ten days to figure out it was missing after he came back.

By then, he'd gotten into an argument with another millwright and thought he'd been the one who stole or hid his toolbox.

The issue went unresolved for the next three months, and Rocky had pretty much written it off and decided he'd order a new box and replacement tools when he got around to it.

"It will be nice to take a brand-new box full of unused tools home when I retire anyhow," thought Rocky.

And then one day, the facilities crew came through and completed a relamping project in the area Rocky's office was in.

The first morning it was lit, Rocky was drinking coffee and admiring what a difference the new, more powerful lamps made.

He could see further up into the steel than had ever been possible.

He tipped his coffee all the way back and his eyes came to rest on the red wheels of his toolbox, twenty-eight feet above where it had been sitting on the floor.

When he cut it loose the following weekend, Rocky found out that Rob was actually a pretty good welder.

A POWERFUL ATTITUDE ADJUSTMENT

"Don't expect an A in my class," Kiven Dodd told the group of apprentices seated at the blueprint drawing tables.

"Most college classes for skilled trades are blow-off classes where you get an A just for having a pulse and showing up. But here's the deal," he snapped. "There's no easy A in my class."

"This is some welcome speech," Skip Hendrich thought to himself.

Class hadn't even been in session five minutes on the first night and this instructor was laying the smackdown on a room full of people he'd just met.

This was going to be a long fifteen weeks.

Kiven Dodd continued.

"The majority of you lazy asses wouldn't even show up if you didn't need the attendance sheet to get paid. Yeah, I know you get paid for coming to class, and I also know you rarely stay all night."

"Some of you think you can leave on break and not come back. Go ahead and try that here. I'll fail you and recommend you be thrown out of the apprenticeship program."

Skip looked over at Jake Sample, then at the rest of the room.

Every student was sitting straight up in their desks, focused intently on the quirky little man at the front of the room.

Both Skip and Jake had a 4.0 grade point average, and neither was willing to risk ruining it by making this guy mad the first night.

But Skip could tell this wasn't going to be easy.

Like many of the other instructors in the skilled trades program at the local college, Kiven Dodd was a tradesman from the plant who worked as an adjunct.

A tool and die-maker by trade, he was assigned to the central tool room, a stand-alone tool shop where the site's big jobs were handled.

Historically, tool and die-makers were paid a quarter more an hour than the other trades, and many considered themselves to be better than the rest.

This was obvious with Kiven Dodd in the way he spoke to the 'lesser' trades.

"You millwrights just do the best you can," he quipped.

Another time he said, "I don't know why pipefitters are in here anyhow. The only thing they need to know is shit runs downhill. You don't need a blueprint for that, you just need a level…"

Skip and Jake made it to every class that semester and put up with Kiven's ego without incident.

They were in good shape by the last night, as they'd aced all their tests and had done all their homework and extra credit.

At the end of the night, they were handed a sheet with their final grade.

Skip couldn't believe his eyes.

Despite the fact that every column across the entire sheet of paper had an "A" in it, the very last column – the one labeled "Overall Grade" held a big fat B+.

"What's this?" Skip demanded out loud.

Kiven walked over and put his hand on Skip's desk.

"That's the grade you earned in this class. I think you did pretty good for a millwright." Kiven said smugly.

"How did my overall grade fall to a B+ if everything along the way was an A or better?" Skip pointed out.

"You missed a couple of questions on the exam. Not enough to drop your grade, but combined with your lack of participation in class projects..."

"Lack of participation? Are you kidding me? I jumped through all your hoops and did all your ridiculous extra credit. If anyone earned an A, it was me."

Skip slammed his book, picked up his backpack, and left early without filling out the course evaluation form.

If he never laid eyes on the jerk who ruined his college four point again, that would be just fine with him.

Over the next week, Skip called the skilled trades director at the college to see if anything could be done about his grade.

There had only been two A's given out in the class – both to tool and die apprentices who had worked with Kiven in the tool room.

Although it was revealing that Jake had the exact same grade pattern as Skip, the director said grades were ultimately controlled by the individual instructor and it would take an act of God or better to have them amended without his assistance.

Unfortunately, that was completely out of the question.

Kiven would never go back and give Skip a better grade after he'd walked out of his classroom early the last night.

He'd called the director the next day trying to have Skip's pay docked, but the director had let it slide after hearing Skip's side of the story.

Besides, this wasn't the first complaint he'd had about Kiven Dodd's grading practices.

A week later, Skip looked across the break table at Jake, then back down at the semester report he'd received in the mail the day before.

The 4.0 that had owned the Cumulative GPA column was now replaced by a 3.89.

Skip was mad as hell.

"I never wanted a four point in high school. I started off pretty rough my freshman year and pulled it up to graduate with a 3.2."

"But I just kind of always thought I'd have a four point in college because it seemed a shame not to keep it up after I started out so strong."

"I know," Jake agreed. "I thought the same thing."

"This isn't over," Skip pledged.

"I'll pick you up tomorrow at the start of lunch," Skip told Jake. "We'll go for a ride."

The next day at lunch, the pair went to see Lisa Swift, who was assigned to the department next to the tool room.

"He sits alone at that same picnic table every day. He lays his lunch things out like a person with deep personal issues. He's so neat and organized. It's sad and kind of weird," Lisa said softly.

Skip didn't care how sad a life Kiven Dodd lived.

This guy was single-handedly responsible for messing up Skip's four point, and he'd done it deliberately.

He had to pay.

"Are you staying over tonight?" Skip asked Jake.

"Yeah, we're changing out some barrels in the blast room," Jake replied.

"Show up at that picnic table at 5 pm," Skip told Jake as he dropped him back off.

When Jake arrived at the picnic table later that day, he didn't see Skip anywhere.

"Hey! Up here!" Skip said from above.

Jake looked straight up and saw Skip's head peering over the side of the roof thirty-five feet above.

"Slide that picnic table just off the concrete and up against the building and stand back," Skip ordered.

Jake did what he was told, and Skip dumped a bucket of water over the edge of the roof.

It hit a little off-center of the table and splashed out into the lawn.

"OOHH! I like it!" Jake laughed.

"Now slide it back and come give me a hand," Skip directed.

Jake came out the roof hatch just in time to see Skip dump two buckets of water into a big yellow trash can he'd set by the spot he'd marked near the edge of the roof.

The two disgruntled apprentices carried more than forty gallons of water across the roof that evening preparing for their high-volume hit.

"Act of God," thought Skip. "I'll show 'em an act of God!"

Now all they had to do was wait.

The following day just before lunch, Jake drove his cart around the side of the plant, walked to the picnic table, and dragged it into position.

He went back to his cart and drove it around to the ladder behind the plant.

This is where they'd make their getaway.

Skip was in position as Jake arrived at the yellow barrel.

To their dismay, Kiven took one look at the table, set his food down, and dragged it back onto the concrete slab.

"Dang it," huffed Skip.

He'd thought about dumping the barrel when Kiven had stood in front, but that would have been a messy, ineffective hit.

"I'm working over tonight. I'll have a lock there tomorrow to keep it in place," he said.

The next day, Jake dragged the table over to the pipe Skip had driven into the ground.

A chain and lock lay attached to it in the grass, so he snapped the lock around the base of the table and hustled back to his cart.

About ten minutes later, Kiven discovered his picnic table had been moved once again.

"It's probably the guy who sits at that other table," Kiven thought.

They'd had words a few weeks back, and they hadn't been nice ones.

Kiven set his lunch down and gave the table a tug, but this time it didn't budge.

He heard the chain clank against the pipe on the bottom and discovered the lock.

He backed up, put his hands on his hips, and thought about where he was going to eat.

Since this was the only available picnic table, he decided he'd have to sit here until he could have the lock cut off.

He climbed on the bench facing the plant and organized his lunch as good as he could on the tilted surface.

He opened his square container and took out his sandwich.

As he took his first bite, a tidal wave of water smashed into the center of the picnic table and shot outward with unbelievable force.

The blast picked him off the bench and hurled him backwards into the grass, sending him sliding down an incline while rolling from side to side.

I'm not sure if it was the water hitting him or him hitting the ground that knocked the wind out of him, but he gasped for air like a fish on land twenty-five feet from where he'd sat down.

Lunch items, glasses, and the rest of Kiven's belongings were scattered about, totally drenched and discombobulated from being water-bombed.

Fortunately for Skip and Jake, Kiven was one of those guys who had so many arguments going on at once that there was no chance of figuring out who did it.

A LITTLE GOES A LONG WAY

When Biff Buffman first started as line-side supervisor, he was out to make a name for himself, and it wasn't a very good one.

He'd written half a dozen people up for coming back from break 30 seconds late, even though the bathrooms near the line were closed and they'd had to walk to the locker room to relieve themselves.

When it came time for the team's weekly meeting, he cancelled it and made them stay on the line to make up the lost production.

This didn't make Frankie Ford happy at all.

Team meetings were held so members could voice their job-related concerns, receive updates about ongoing issues, and take a break from the line.

This was not Biff Buffman's production time.

This was the team's time.

Biff shrugged when Frankie brought this up.

"Tell your teammates to come back from break on time and I won't have to cancel your meetings," he retorted. "And if they don't, your breaks will be next."

As you might imagine, this answer didn't sit well with Frankie.

He especially despised that Biff was trying to turn part of the team against the others because of a problem management had created when they closed a bathroom.

Frankie went to talk with the others, and the next day, every single one of them was two minutes late from break as they walked back from the locker room together.

Biff was losing his mind by the time the group returned.

"I'll write every single one of you up for this!" he threatened.

"You might want to think about writing the people up who are supposed to be fixing our bathrooms," Frankie advised.

Biff stormed off to the front of the plant and the line ran until lunch with nobody getting written up or even talked to.

But when the group got back from lunch, all the radios on the line were gone.

As they started to complain about their music being taken away, Biff got out his contract book and opened it to the page he'd marked.

"Shop Rule 21: All radios must be battery-operated and no larger than 8 x 10 inches in size," he recited.

"You'd better inform the other departments," Frankie growled. "We've had those radios since you were in diapers. Get me a committeeman."

The rest of the afternoon didn't go well on the assembly line.

People pull out every trick in the book to cause downtime when they're mad, and Biff got to experience rebellion on a wider scale than ever before.

When the team walked out the door that day, afternoon production was less than a quarter of what it was supposed to have been.

The next morning when the team arrived at work, all the chairs in the break area had been removed and hard metal benches sat in their place.

"You're really not that smart, are you Buffy?" Frankie asked openly. "You're about to find out what happens to bad bosses."

"Just run the line," Biff ordered, as he pointed to Frankie's station.

"You got it, boss," Frankie saluted, as he marched into position.

The line didn't run very well again that morning.

As he left for first break, Frankie said, "Keep these numbers up and you'll be looking for a different job. The plant manager isn't going to put up with lost production."

"The plant manager is well aware that you guys are deliberately slowing down production." Biff shot back.

"Yes, but does he know you're the problem?" Frankie inquired.

Frankie didn't wait around for an answer.

He took off for the tool and die area.

Frankie was on a mission.

He came back from break and worked until lunch.

Frankie stayed next to the line as Biff and the others walked away, then he slipped into Biff's office unnoticed.

About half an hour after lunch, Biff came out of his office to make his rounds to check production.

Things were running better than they had that morning.

"See, I told you the people would fall into line," Biff scoffed as he walked past Frankie's station.

Frankie smiled, pointed at Biff, and said, "Uh, you've got a little something on the side of your face."

Biff reached up to wipe the spot where Frankie had pointed and looked down at his hand as he pulled it away.

"What the...?!" Biff said out loud, as he examined his bright blue palm.

He rubbed his fingers together, and the thin, grease-like substance spread across his entire hand almost magically.

He touched the other side of his face with his other hand and came away clean.

"Ooh, you got some in your ear, too. And your hair," Frankie cooed.

Biff spun and ran for the roll of paper towels on the break table.

He ripped a couple off and started rubbing the side of his face.

"Keep going! I think you've almost got it all!" Frankie hollered.

(Of course, he did this to draw everyone's attention to Biff.)

Biff's eyes got wide as he pulled the paper towel away from the side of his face.

Not only was the paper towel completely blue, but the back of his hand was now almost completely blue as well.

He threw the paper towel in the trash and rushed to the birdbath sink just outside the break area.

He tried to see the side of his face in the dirty little mirror bolted to the column, but it was caked with old soap scum.

He ripped off a towel, wet it down, and started wiping the mirror off with one hand as he put soap on another to use to clean his face.

The little mirror didn't clean up very well, but Biff was able to see that a third of his head was blue on one side.

He dipped his head in the water and scrubbed soap on the side of his face with both hands.

The bubbles got blue and stayed that way for minutes.

After a little while and a lot more soap, the bubbles turned white again.

But to Biff's utter dismay, his hands stayed blue.

Granted, they were a lighter shade of blue than they had been, but they were definitely, undeniably stained a prominent shade of blue.

His eyeball bugged as he strained to see the side of his face in the grubby little mirror.

The whole side of his head was still blue, too.

"What the...?!" Biff stammered, as he dabbed at his arm with a new piece of paper towel.

"Is this some kind of...paint?!?" he wondered aloud.

This time, the paper towel stayed white.

About this time, Biff looked up and noticed that the line had stopped and most of the crew was looking at him.

"GET BACK TO WORK!" he screamed and ran into his office.

He came out a few minutes later holding his disconnected office phone at arm's length in front of him like a dead animal.

Blue dye covered the ear and mouth pieces.

He dropped the phone in the trash, went back in his office, locked up, and left.

Biff's face and hands were still blue the next day.

Rumor had it he'd tried lacquer thinner, mineral spirits, and even toilet bowl cleaner to no avail.

The engineers up front figured (correctly so) that someone had put blue Dykem (steel marking dye) on his office phone.

"There's no way to get it out. It just has to wear off," they told him, (which wasn't entirely true).

"You're looking pretty rough these days, Buffy," Frankie giggled, as Biff patrolled the line.

A few days later, one of the die makers told Biff about Dykem remover (literally the ONLY thing that takes Dykem off) and Buffy's blues went away...

FILL 'ER UP!

From the first day they'd met, Hal Dobber and Rob Robeson didn't like each other.

Unfortunately, this didn't matter to the company that needed them to work together to fix broken machines.

Most days they rose above their differences and did a good job.

But on certain days they wanted to knock each other out.

Rob was a brute of a man who resembled a large lumberjack.

He had a big gut, forearms as thick as thighs, and calves like tree trunks.

(I watched him pick a 400-pound transformer off a flatbed cart and set it on the workbench behind him with his bare hands without making a sound one day.)

He wasn't the sort of guy you'd want to fight, and Hal Dobber knew it.

This, however, did not change the fact that Hal hated Rob's guts and wasn't afraid of him.

Hal had fired the first shot when he used concrete anchors to bolt Rob's toolbox to the floor where it sat.

As big and strong as Rob was, the big dummy couldn't budge his box from where it was anchored.

The next day, Hal went to unlock his toolbox, and all his locks had been greased.

He took his time cleaning it up and immediately returned the favor – except he used superglue on all of Rob's locks.

Even the ones on his locker.

Rob had to replace all the locks, as they never seem to work right after they're glued one time.

"So, you want to destroy people's toolboxes, huh?" Rob thought out loud.

Sunday rolled around that week, and Hal hadn't been asked to work, but Rob had.

Rob rolled Hal's big toolbox away from the wall, pulled out a drill, and drilled two holes – one top center and another centered halfway down – in the back of Hal's toolbox.

Next, he tapped the holes and blew them out with an air hose.

He whistled a tune as he screwed grease zerks in the holes and tightened them with a crescent wrench.

Now the only thing left to do was roll the 55-gallon drum of grease over, hook the air hose up to the pneumatic pump, and fill 'er up.

The drawers wiggled and swelled as the grease made its way through.

He shut the pump off as the thick, brown menace began oozing from between the drawers in front.

He moved the grease line to the other zerk and began the process again.

This time, when the grease began oozing out the front, he pushed against it with a towel until he couldn't hold it in anymore.

He took the grease barrel back and grabbed a big box of rags to clean up the mess.

He wiped it all down, then used a flathead screwdriver to dig the rest of the grease from between the drawers so you'd swear nothing could be wrong.

He pushed the heavy box back against the wall and went home.

It was 6:30 the next morning when Hal stuck his key in to open his toolbox.

He removed the padlock and lifted the bar that held the drawers in the locked position.

He grabbed the top left drawer to open it so he could throw his keys and his padlock in like he always did.

At first, the drawer didn't seem to want to move, but he pulled hard and it slowly broke loose.

As he labored to pull it out, he didn't seem to understand what was going on.

His box had double roller slides on the drawers.

It wasn't one of those metal-on-metal jobs.

It still didn't feel right, like he was fighting the cylinder on a screen door.

He pulled it out further and it got easier still.

Once it reached the end, he saw the back half had been filled with grease.

"What the??" he wondered.

His heart dropped as he looked below at the other drawers that were now being pushed out because of the grease.

"Good one," he thought, as he shoved the locking bar back into place.

He hopped on a fork truck, scooped up the box, and drove to an undisclosed location.

His box showed back up a few days later like nothing had ever happened.

Chapter Six

That's Bound to Leave a Mark!

While it's not polite to make fun when someone gets hurt, it's perfectly acceptable to mess with them once you know they're ok.

THE CRIME SCENE

"Hey Kid, can you weld this bracket up for me?" Donny Tompkins asked.

He startled me, as there had been no one around when I'd dropped my hood to burn another stick of rod.

"Sure," I said, as I stepped down from the ladder and pulled the ground clamp.

"It'll be good to get away from this beast for a minute," I said.

I clamped the ground to the table where he'd laid the bracket and turned the heat down so I wouldn't burn through the thinner iron.

He stood on his toes and examined the welds on the chute I'd been building.

"Looks like you're getting the hang of burning rod, Kid."

"You'll have it all figured out by the time you journey out."

Donny was a good millwright.

I'd been assigned to work with him a few weeks earlier, and he'd shown me some tricks that had really helped me out.

"What are you working on today?" I asked.

"I'm building support brackets for the electricians, then I've got to bolt down some panel boxes and conveyors," he replied.

Donnie was always on the move.

He talked fast, he walked fast, and he had a quick sense of humor.

I dropped my hood, made four quick welds, and Donnie was on his way.

"Careful, that's hot!" I said, as he smiled and grabbed it by the cool end.

"Thanks, Kid," he nodded, as he whirled around to leave.

"Watch it!" I shouted, but my warning was too late.

His forehead collided with the corner of the chute I'd been building, and the force of the blow took his feet out from under him.

He fell too fast for me to catch him, but I was able to grab the hot bracket from his hand so it didn't land on his face.

I tossed it to the side as the heat started burning through my glove and took a step toward where he was now lying on his back.

As I leaned in to look at him, my raised welding hood hit the corner he'd ran into and flew backwards, bouncing across the floor.

A trickle of blood started down the side of his face, but his eyes were open, and he didn't seem disoriented.

He scrambled to get up, but another millwright named Jerry ran up and told him to stay down.

"I'm ok," Donny stammered as he reached up to touch his head.

He winced in pain and jerked his hand away, and a big squirt of blood shot out and ran down his nose.

I hustled over to the sink, ripped a three-foot chunk of paper towel off the roll, and handed it to him as he pulled himself to his feet.

"Let's go see the nurse," Jerry said as he grabbed Donnie by the arm and pulled him toward his cart.

A small crowd had started to gather as they rode off down the aisle.

"Is your chute ok," another millwright named Dan joked.

"Yeah, it's pretty sturdy," I answered, leaning against the table.

"Are you ok?" Dan asked, noticing I was a few shades lighter than usual.

"That was a lot of blood," I said weakly.

"I don't really like the sight of blood," I grimaced.

"Yeah, head wounds always bleed a lot," he said. "C'mon, let's get some air."

We hopped on his cart and headed for the back door of the plant.

The fresh air and sunshine felt good after welding all morning, and we sat out by the coils of steel for fifteen minutes or so.

"Let's go check on Donny," Dan said.

We pulled up in front of medical just as Jerry was pulling away.

"He's going to be ok, but he's got a pretty good gash on his forehead," Jerry informed us.

We looked through the window and saw Donnie leaned back in the exam chair.

The nurse had a huge band aid in her hand and was trying to figure out the best position to stick it so it wouldn't interfere with Donnie's facial features.

She settled on a diagonal application that spanned from his left temple to the hairline above his right eye.

"C'mon Kid, let's go," Dan said.

He didn't say much as we took off down the aisle toward the millwright shop.

My heart sank as we pulled in and saw the yellow caution tape that had been strung up around my hopper job.

Two hand-written paper signs hung from the tape that said, "CRIME SCENE."

"Am I in trouble?" I asked him. "Should I have had it taped off while I was building it in the shop?"

"It wouldn't have mattered," Dan reasoned. "He'd have to have gone inside your tape to have you weld his bracket. He knew the hopper was there."

"You'll be fine" he said, as he hopped off the cart and walked to the row of lockers along the wall.

As I got off the cart and walked toward the hopper, I could smell bleach coming from the mop bucket next to the taped-off area.

The blood had been cleaned up and a big fan was drying the floor where the incident had occurred.

Brad Porter was just getting up from kneeling at the spot where Donnie had landed.

At first, I'd imagined he'd been praying, but then I saw a thick piece of white chalk in his hand and noticed the body outline on the floor.

The crime scene drawing of Donnie had one leg bent in a funny position, a goofy look on its face, two X's for eyes, and stars flying around its head.

Just when I thought it couldn't get any better, Dan walked up and placed a big band-aid on the forehead in the same position as the one we'd seen the nurse stick on Donnie.

It was break time when Donnie returned to the scene of the crime, and the whole crew had a good laugh at his expense, just like factory families do.

HOT LIPS

In Biff Buffman's opinion, the union was the worst thing that ever happened to the automotive industry.

He liked screwing with specific groups of people for the purpose of causing trouble for the committeemen who represented them.

One day, Biff came strolling into the union office with a shit-eating grin on his face.

He'd blocked an inter-plant transfer when he found out the employee was Danny Goodman's nephew, and he thought he'd stop by to let Danny know in person.

"I'm already three steps over your head, Buffy," the shop committeeman said, as he set his phone on the receiver. "Labor's calling me back in five minutes."

"It won't matter," Biff shrugged. "I can't let him go. There's nobody trained to take over his job, and I can't be in the hole while somebody else learns."

Biff walked over to the coffee pot in the corner, grabbed a foam cup off the stack, and filled it with water.

"You've had three months to train a replacement for that job. You should have done it when the fill-in guy filed his training request form. Instead, you chose to screw around," Danny shot back.

Biff looked down at the floor and wondered if the back-up guy really did have a valid training request form on file.

Even if he did, labor would probably give him at least a few more weeks.

Biff drained the cup of water, filled it back up, and grabbed a plastic lid.

He knew this drove the committeemen crazy, as they all kicked in and bought coffee supplies for the people they represented in the plant.

Buffy was NOT one of their people.

A few weeks before, a district committeeman hollered at Biff for drinking from a cup and immediately throwing it away, so Biff childishly grabbed a new one and did it again.

Since then, he'd slammed a water and taken a free to-go cup with a lid every time he came into their office.

This time would be no different – or so he thought.

He opened the flap on the lid and set the cup on the desk as a woman fork truck driver walked past him to the coffee pot.

Just as he started to speak, the phone rang.

Danny picked up the receiver and listened for a minute.

"He's here now. Can I put you on speaker?" he asked, as the woman filled two cups with coffee, put lids on, and set them on the desk.

Danny hit a button and set the phone back down.

"Biff? Can you hear me?" the head of labor relations said.

"Uh, yeah," Biff said, completely caught off guard.

He'd expected the plant labor rep to handle this issue, not the big guy from divisional.

"Biff, you're going to let that young man go to his new job. I got a call from the plant manager over there and they need to start training the new team members to ramp-up their new product line."

"I promised him I'd get people right away. There's no reason your guy can't get started next week, is there?" the old boy demanded.

"No, if that's the case, I'll have to make do with what I've got," Biff replied.

Danny grinned in Biff's face as they exchanged goodbyes and hung up.

"You lose again, Buffy," Danny crowed. "Now get out of my office!"

Biff spun, grabbed the cup off the desk, and tipped it like he was slamming a beer.

As the rush of liquid hit his mouth, he let out a scream and blew coffee all over the wall.

"That's my coffee!" the fork truck driver complained.

Buffy spiked the cup in the sink and cranked on the cold water.

He hit his head on the shelf when he tried to get his lips under the tap.

When he still couldn't reach, he frantically started scooping water into his mouth with his hand.

After about a minute, he ripped off a paper towel and put it over his face before running out the office door.

He was off the rest of the day and that weekend, but his lips were still red and swollen on Monday.

Although his injury only lasted a few weeks, the nickname "Hot Lips" stuck with him for six months before he stumbled upon a better one.

WALK OF SHAME

My most embarrassing factory moment (to date) began in a dimly lit corner of plant three on a Saturday morning in the late nineties.

DID YOU GET ONE OF THESE YET TODAY?

About 9:30 am, Brad Porter, Jerry Shoultes, and I were assigned to weld support brackets under a conveyor system that had buckled due to being overloaded.

The department we were working in was next to the automatics, which were notorious for spraying oil mist in the air 24/7.

(Thinking back, it's amazing to me that security wrote burn permits in some of those areas at all.)

The floors were slippery and dangerous, transitioning from worn grating over the pits to concrete and back to smooth, slick steel in places.

The roller conveyor system that sat on top of the whole mess was used to transport trays of parts from one machining operation to the next.

Because I was the apprentice, it was me who had to crawl around in the places that were hard to fit into.

I didn't mind it though.

I was an eager apprentice back then.

(A lot has changed in thirty years.)

It took about an hour to clamp our supports in place and stretch out our welding cables.

Jerry Shoultes pulled his leather sleeves over his green coveralls, then put on his heavy welder's gloves as I headed for the inside of the line.

BRANDY BOOTH

Millwrights didn't do their own welding back then, so we were assigned the same thin blue coveralls that most regular maintenance men wore in the nineties.

The problem was – apprentice millwrights had 160 hours of welding hours to fill in to attain their journeyman's card, and Jerry Shoultes thought this was the perfect opportunity for an apprentice to learn in the field.

(He really just didn't want to go under those conveyors, but like I said, I didn't mind.)

Jerry got the easy welds on the top and aisle side of the conveyors, and I worked on the inside of the line and crawled underneath to get the tight spots.

I was wedged in between where two conveyors merged together when my morning took a turn I'll never forget.

As it would turn out, those thin blue coveralls go up like dry newspaper if you dip a pantleg in oil and weld for a minute without noticing you're on fire.

About the time the heat made its way up to my armpit, I heard Jerry yell.

When I lifted my hood, my whole right side was engulfed.

"THE KID'S ON FIRE!" Jerry hollered to Brad who was near the back of the weld buggy.

I threw my stinger and hood to the side and whirled to look for the quickest way out of the conveyor I was caught in between.

There was no room to stop, drop, and roll like I'd been taught in grade school.

Besides, that would have just oiled me up and stoked the already large fire.

In a split second, I decided the quickest way out was to jump over the conveyor and roll out into the aisle.

I wasn't quite on top of the conveyor when the stream from Brad's water fire extinguisher hit me in the neck and danced up and down my side.

I slipped and landed on my butt on top of the rollers but quickly spun my body around so Brad could hose the remaining hot spots.

The entire right leg of my coveralls was gone clear up to my armpit.

Jerry ran over to help me off the aisle side of the conveyor.

As he guided me down, my foot slipped in the wet oil and my coveralls ripped all the way around my middle as he saved me from hitting the floor.

They helped me up, and I held my arms out to my sides.

The lower half of my coveralls was hanging by a thread around back, and the only thing I had on underneath was my underwear and boots.

A crackly, melted cuff around my ankle was all that was left of my right pant leg.

Miraculously, the only thing that hurt was the leg I'd scraped while trying to hop up on the conveyor when I was fully ablaze.

Other than that, there were a couple red spots where the coverall material had melted like candle wax and stuck to my thigh.

"I'm alright, but I'll need new coveralls. These ones have a smoking problem," I quipped.

"Go sit on the cart while we roll these leads up and we'll take you to the locker room," Brad instructed.

I saw them talking as they rolled up the cables, but I couldn't hear what they were saying.

"Hey Kid, come here for a second," Jerry said from the back of the cart.

I hopped off the cart and walked back to see what the old boy needed.

When I got there, he said "I just want to check and see..."

Without warning, he bent down, grabbed the lower half of my coveralls, and yanked my left foot right out from underneath me.

I threw my arms in the air thinking I was going straight down on my back, but to my surprise, Brad was there to catch me.

(Notice I didn't say he was there to help me.)

As Jerry pulled at what was left of my bottoms, Brad grabbed what was left of the top half and stripped me clean with one huge tug.

As my whitey tighties touched down on the oily floor, Jerry dragged me down the center of the aisle away from the cart.

I'd been fighting to keep what was left of those coveralls, but it wasn't worth being dragged for miles on my butt down an oily floor.

After about twenty feet, I worked my ankle and toe free and slid to a stop.

Jerry ran back past me and hopped on the cart where Brad was playing getaway driver.

I jumped to my feet and ran after them a little way, but then the thought occurred to me that they'd drive me around to show me off if I did catch them.

My mind raced to think of a route back to the locker room without being seen, but the section of the plant between me and the locker room was assembly lines from wall to wall.

I looked for rags, a fig leaf, or anything else I could use to cover myself, but the place was as bare as I was.

I hustled down a side aisle and slid between the big packs of dunnage stacked three high.

As I came out from between the rows of dunnage, I startled a woman who was sorting parts at a little table.

I must have looked pretty goofy standing there in my charred underwear and work boots, but I'm sure she could see by the look on my face that I hadn't done it on purpose.

She'd looked a little surprised at first but didn't say anything as I hustled past.

I wasn't stopping to answer questions anyway.

As I looked over my shoulder to verify she was still looking at me, I caught sight of the back of my previously white underwear.

Without going into too much detail, things were looking pretty dark and droopy in the rear-view after being dragged down the aisle.

(I'd later discover two golf ball-sized holes in the lower left side that matched the two red marks on my butt.)

A quick look in front of me verified what I'd already known.

There was no way to get to the locker room without passing between two long assembly lines, so I picked the route that would take me out closest to the entrance of the locker room and made a run for it.

I didn't get ten feet down that aisle before workers on both sides pulled the emergency cords to stop the line.

I wanted to die as the hoots, hollers, catcalls, and a few "eew's" came hurdling my way.

Looking back, I'm fortunate that cameras and video cameras weren't as accessible as they are today, so there isn't any photographic evidence of what happened that day.

It seemed like I was jogging in slow motion, but I know I was moving along at a pretty good clip.

The oil had started to wear off my boots, and I was gaining traction.

I tried to avoid eye contact but couldn't help but notice the uncomfortable smiles and other awkward expressions I saw on the faces of the people nearest the aisle.

"Is he bleeding?" I heard one woman say.

I kicked it up a gear and sprinted straight to my locker in the back corner of the locker room.

I looked in all directions to see if I had company.

Realizing I didn't, I unlocked my combination lock and headed for the shower.

I was a little beat up in places, but I'd learned to keep an extra change of clothes for when I showered at the end of the day.

Needless to say, I showered early and found a good hiding spot.

Jerry Shoultes and Brad Porter searched but never found me until the next morning.

"You ok, Kid? We went to get help, but when we came back, you were gone," they explained.

"Sure, you did..."

BACK-DOOR BULLSEYE

Smart apprentices paid attention to where all the water sources were located in each factory, because they'd become prime targets when it came time to rotate.

Andy Carrier knew this better than anyone.

He'd been getting wet every six months for the last three years.

Now he was just one rotation away from having enough hours to complete his apprenticeship.

About a week before rotation, he started taking a different way each time he came in or out of the plant.

This frustrated a couple of senior journeymen who had their traditional hits set up in places he knew to stay away from.

Charlie Sagebrush and Herb Verlenbeck had played too many of the same tricks on the other apprentices, and word had gotten back to Andy about their hit locations and techniques.

He wasn't about to walk into anyone's silly old trap.

What he'd really like to do was punch out of this plant for the last time a dry apprentice.

With three days left to go, Andy was working in the millwright shop when a shadow on the floor moved.

He backed up to get a better look, and five gallons of water hit the floor where he'd been standing.

He jumped backwards and looked up at the skylight, but his attacker was gone.

Now, with only two days left, it was time to call in an expert.

"He knows how to move around so we can't get him," Herb explained to Chip "Buckshot" Flanerty.

Buckshot knew exactly what Herb meant.

A lot of cagey targets had tried to escape Buckshot's wrath, but he'd gotten every single one of them.

Every. Single. One.

DID YOU GET ONE OF THESE YET TODAY?

Buckshot was famously known for shimmying up a building column with a rope tied to his belt, pulling up a five-gallon pail of water, and dumping it on another famous water thrower who had no idea there was danger lurking in the darkness above.

He didn't charge for a hit, but everyone knew he'd gladly accept a twelve pack – or a case if the job was big enough.

"We don't really want to get him wet in a dark corner of the plant," Charlie Sagebrush explained.

"We'd rather it happened in front of everyone, preferably first thing in the morning or at break time," Herb added.

"He steers clear of all the water sources," Charlie said. "He takes a different route to his toolbox to put on his boots every morning."

"Show me where he puts his boots on."

They walked to the millwright area and Buckshot looked under the table across from the row of toolboxes and foot lockers lined up against the back wall.

"If he knows where all the water sources are, you fellas need a water cannon," Buckshot reasoned.

"A water cannon is a sealed PVC pipe filled with water and pressurized by air. I can mount it up under the table and run a ripcord under the benches to the break table," he planned.

"That should do the trick," Charlie nodded.

He looked over at Herb, who was grinning from ear to ear.

"It will be ready to go by morning," Buckshot promised.

BRANDY BOOTH

The next morning, Andy entered the plant from a side door behind the millwright area.

"He must have walked all the way around the plant from the gate," marveled Herb.

Andy hesitated before creeping the rest of the way to his box, carefully examining the trades at the break table and scanning the area above for buckets, hoses, and other water-delivery tools.

Seeing none, he set his lunch box down and bent down to get his boots.

From out of nowhere, a powerful stream of water blasted Andy in the backside, nearly propelling him over the top of his footlocker and into the concrete wall.

He pushed himself backwards, but his tennis shoes slipped on the wet floor, causing him to slide down, then roll off to the side.

He ran five steps and turned to watch the stream pound his footlocker for another ten seconds before it petered out.

Andy groaned as he looked under the table and saw the water cannon.

He noticed the handle and followed the ripcord down the line of work benches to the break table where the millwrights were sitting.

The cord ended at Herb Verlenbeck's chair.

As Andy looked up, Herb leaned back and shot him in the chin with a stream of water from the "silver salute" (water fire extinguisher) bottle hidden behind his chair.

"We missed the top half the first time, but you're good now," he laughed.

BURNIN' FOR YOU!

Every guy in the plant wanted to date Lisa Swift.

The new apprentice was beautiful, smart, and driven - but that wasn't the first thing most men noticed about her.

A few years before Lisa was put on trades, she'd purchased a new pair of boobs, which she didn't mind showing off with low-cut tops on hot summer days.

One day, Lisa was assigned to drill holes in the concrete to anchor a new office wall.

Every time she bent down to drill another hole, Francis "Rocky" Boulderock would slide up and stand over her, trying to look down her shirt.

She stopped when she'd noticed him the first few times, but he wouldn't leave so she turned her back to him and kept drilling.

Rocky had been married for forty years and openly admitted that his wife didn't like him at all, which didn't surprise anyone who knew him.

Although he was in his sixties, he still lifted weights three times a week and was in better than decent shape.

As Rocky swayed back and forth in his skin-induced trance, the big hammer drill began to buck and jerk, nearly sending Lisa to the floor.

She fought to hold on and keep drilling, but the bit hopped up and down, stuttered a few times, and locked up tight.

The clutch on the drill made a grinding sound, and she jerked it up sharply three times before she gave up and let go.

"Stuck again?" Rocky asked in his John Wayne voice as he set his clipboard down.

"Yes. Another rebar. That's the third one in a row," Lisa said, as she turned her back and tugged at her coveralls.

Rocky pushed up his sleeves, puffed out his chest, and grabbed the drill by the handle.

He pulled hard and nearly tipped on his face.

After righting himself, he said something under his breath, rubbed his hands together, and gave it another go.

This time he jerked the drill up, let it back down slowly, and jerked it hard again, as hammer drills are designed to do.

The bit wouldn't budge.

He quickened his pace, jerking faster and harder, which caused his hair and glasses to slide to the point of barely hanging on.

The bit was mocking him now.

He became more aggressive with every furious tug, grunting and over-flexing as white droplets of spit spritzed the scene from the corner of his mouth.

After twenty healthy jerks, the bit finally broke free.

Lisa thanked him, grabbed the drill, and went straight back at the unfinished hole.

She eased the tip in so it wouldn't get caught in the same groove as before, then increased the pressure slowly and steadily as she'd been taught.

Rocky hovered over her, hugging his clipboard and staring at her cleavage in case she needed his help again.

Lisa drilled for a long time, but the metal rebar wouldn't surrender.

She finally grew tired and stopped, but Rocky wasn't paying attention and thought she'd gotten the bit stuck again.

The moment she stood up, he grabbed the handle and gave it a big heroic yank.

Because it wasn't stuck, the drill flew up with such force that it nearly took him over backwards.

He swung his arms to regain his balance, and the cord flew up and nearly hit Lisa in the back of the head.

She hadn't noticed his goofy dance because her hammer's handle had twisted in her tool belt and became lodged in the back pocket of her coveralls when she'd stood up.

She was tangled up good and looking the other way.

Rocky regained his composure and turned to hand her the drill.

But instead of handing it to her normally, he tried to be a macho man and grabbed it by the bit so she could take the drill by the handle, like an expert might hand someone a gun or a knife.

Unfortunately, the drill was hot from where she'd hit the rebar and it started burning his hand.

He held it out farther hoping she'd grab it, but her tool belt wasn't giving up the fight.

He started to dance around, but the tough guy inside wouldn't allow him to drop it or change his grip to a cooler spot.

He tried shaking the drill in front of her to get her attention.

No dice.

When he couldn't stand it anymore, he jammed the handle hard into her side, forcing her to grab it or risk being hit again.

She grabbed it without looking at him, tossed the big drill to the ground, and went back to fighting to free herself.

When he saw she'd turned away, he started dancing around, shaking and blowing on his burnt hand.

His eyes got big when he stopped moving it long enough to examine it, and he went running for the drinking fountain on the wall across the room.

THE EYE INJURY

About ten days after I rotated to a new plant, my journeyman and I got a call just after lunch to see if we could unjam and repair an electric furnace.

Unfortunately, I was relatively skinny in those days, so I was chosen to crawl inside the small, dusty space to locate and fix the problem.

DID YOU GET ONE OF THESE YET TODAY?

There was barely enough room to fit, but I squeezed in, dislodged the stuck tray, and filed the damaged brick down so parts could flow through again.

The job turned out to be relatively easy, but some tiny chunks of brick dust had fallen from the ceiling, bounced on the inside of my glasses, and landed in my right eye.

It was close to quitting time when we finished up, so I rinsed it out as good as I could, put my tools away, and went home.

I could still feel debris in my eye that evening, so I rinsed it again and went to bed.

We were working ten-hour shifts at the time, so my alarm was set for 3:45 am to allow me to be to work by 5.

When I woke up the next morning, I immediately knew something was wrong.

I hopped out of bed, made my way to the bathroom, and groaned when I saw myself in the mirror.

My right eye was completely swollen shut and oozing a milky green substance.

I took some ibuprofen, jumped in the shower, and did my best to get my angry eye to calm down.

Although I was successful in washing the nastiness out and warming it up so I could pry it open with my fingers, it was bright red, and I still couldn't see a thing.

I iced it down for a few minutes and got dressed for work.

"At least I'm in the right plant to have this happen," I thought, as I hopped in my truck to make the one-eyed drive.

Plant three was where the main medical office was for the division.

They had a nurse on-duty around the clock, and I wasn't about to burn a day of vacation because of a work-related injury.

When I walked through the door into medical at 4:55 am, I didn't see anyone behind the desk or in the room.

I saw a sign that said, "Ring Bell for Service", so I reached out to do what it said.

"Don't you dare ring that goddamned bell!!" a voice bellowed from off to my right.

I cranked my head to see where it had come from, but I could only see a partly open door into a room with the lights off.

I thought I could make out the corner of a desk, but I wasn't sure.

"What do you want?" the hidden person demanded.

"I, uh..." I stammered.

"I SAID, WHAT DO YOU WANT?"

"My eye is swollen. Can you take a look at it?" my voice cracked.

"Are you just coming to work? Did you hurt yourself at home and are trying to claim it as a work injury?"

Before I could answer, she growled, "I've never seen you before. Are you even assigned to this plant? WHO ARE YOU?"

"My name is Brandy Booth. I'm a millwright apprentice on day shift, but we're working ten hours. I got something in my eye just before I left yesterday and thought I'd be alright, but when I woke up this morning, it was swollen shut."

I felt exhausted from stringing so many words together.

I was scared and injured, and the forty-minute drive in the dark using my non-dominant eye had been stressful.

She must have had her feet up because I heard two heavy thuds followed by a loud creaking sound. She huffed and groaned as she hoisted herself up.

I searched the darkness but still couldn't see her.

The "Nurse on Duty" whiteboard on the wall next to the door said "EdNith" in messy block letters.

Was it Edna or Edith?

I squinted harder and decided it was probably the latter.

A metal chair skidded across the floor and slammed into the wall, then the door flew open, but the light never came on.

I cocked my head to see better and took a quick step back as she came charging out the door.

My elbow bumped the big bottle of electrolyte mix on the counter, but I caught it before it had a chance to fall on the floor.

This lady was built like a linebacker. Her dirty white smock was far too small, and it said "Bill" on the pocket.

I wondered if Bill was ok.

She tossed an empty yogurt container in the trash next to the counter and wiped her face with her sleeve.

"What plant are you from?" she demanded.

"I'm assigned to plant three," I apologized. "I'm sorry if I disturbed your break."

"I'm not on break," she barked. "Give me your badge."

I fumbled to take my badge off the retractor, and she snatched it out of my hand, nearly yanking my pinky off in the process.

She spun around to walk away, and the retractor shot off my belt, bounced across the counter, and snapped closed as she lumbered toward the wall of movable file cabinets.

After a few minutes of looking, she informed me that I was, in fact, NOT assigned to plant three.

"This is my second week here," I protested. "I just rotated from plant five."

"Who is your boss," she demanded.

She eyed me suspiciously as I strained to remember his name, When it finally came to me, she shook her head in disagreement.

"There's nobody here by that name," she informed me.

I told her I thought he might be new too and gave her the name of the other boss I'd met from the same area.

"What a putz," she grunted.

I wasn't sure if she was referring to him or me.

I considered turning around and going back out the door, but she had my badge, and I couldn't get out the turnstile without it.

She grabbed the swinging door and ordered me into the chair in the first room.

"What did you do to your eye?" she asked.

When I told her, she shook her head like she didn't believe me.

"That couldn't have happened if you really had your safety glasses on," she disputed.

I assured her I did and that my journeyman and boss both saw it happen, and they'd verify it when they came to see me.

She shook her head and pulled a thermometer out of a glass measuring cup with two other thermometers in it.

The cup was half full of a milky brownish liquid that didn't look clean at all.

"Why are you here at five am?" she demanded, as she grabbed a protective covering from a box on the counter.

"I've been starting at five since the middle of last week," I explained.

Her big mitts fumbled as she tried to get the small end open.

"I didn't want my boss and journeyman to think I wasn't coming to work," I continued.

"You just didn't want to give up the overtime," she argued, which was partly true.

I watched as she shoved the thermometer into the plastic protector - and straight through the other end.

I opened my mouth to tell her, but she slapped me on the forehead, forced my head back, and speared the unprotected glass tube deep into the soft tissue under my tongue.

I almost bit the thermometer in two as she let my head snap back.

Something wet and slimy on the side of her uniform brushed up against my ear as she leaned over me to grab the blood pressure cuff.

I lifted my arm to wipe it off, and she growled, "Don't you dare take that thermometer out!"

Her breath hit my face like napalm.

I winced so hard that my eye screamed out in pain.

"What in the world has this woman been eating?" I wondered, as I lowered my arm back down. "What causes breath like that?"

I blinked to remove the tears that had defensively pooled up in my good eye and winced again as I saw her up close for the first time.

DID YOU GET ONE OF THESE YET TODAY?

Nurse Edith was a real-life monster.

She had a wide forehead, dark, sunken eyes that seemed too far apart, and an angry red nose like you'd see on a guy who drinks too much whiskey.

She pulled the thermometer out without looking at it, trapped my forearm in her sweaty armpit, and wrestled the worn-out cuff around my bicep.

The velcro attachment wasn't even close to being straight when she was done, and it fell off as she turned to find a stethoscope.

"Your arm is too small. I'm going to have to find the children's cuff," she insulted.

As she waddled out the door, I heard the main door from the plant open and close.

"Not you again," she brayed. "I don't have time for your nonsense, Kevin. Get back to work!"

"But I just need some aspirin," the weak voice begged.

"We're out. Buy some and keep it in your locker. Now go away. I'm busy," she ordered.

The second cuff she put on me was old, stiff, and way too small.

The rough velcro end folded over against the inside of my bicep and dug into my skin as she fought to pull it tight enough to make the connection.

I didn't dare reach my other hand over to flatten it out.

"She'll figure it out when it comes undone," I reasoned, as she began pumping the rubber ball.

But it didn't come undone.

The sharp edge threatened to slice my arm wide open as the pressure built.

She looked up at the clock, and I quickly reached over and slid my fingers inside to straighten it out.

Of course, it let loose at that exact moment.

"WHAT ARE YOU DOING," she screamed in my face.

"It was folded over against my arm. I was just trying to help," I cried.

"It WASN'T folded over, and I DON'T need your help," she roared, as she deflated it against her chest. "Now hold still!"

She pulled it as tight as a tourniquet and smashed the velcro in place.

Her right hand pumped the ball furiously while her left hand hovered over my swollen eye like she'd strike me if I dared to move again.

I started to squirm as the building pressure threatened to cut off the circulation in the left side of my body.

My mind flashed to a story I'd heard about an animal that chewed off its own limb to free itself from a trap.

Her jaw tightened and her nostrils flared as she fought to squeeze the hardening ball.

I tried to make a muscle to push back, but that only made it feel like my arm bone would disintegrate.

I couldn't stand it anymore.

Just before I reached over to yank it free, she jammed her stethoscope into the pit of my elbow.

She reached for the pressure relief valve but didn't let any pressure out.

My vision started to fade as she took her hand away from the valve to push up the yogurt-stained sleeve that covered her watch.

She wasn't looking away this time.

My swollen face throbbed as my heart filled it with trapped blood.

"This sucks," I thought, as I began to lose consciousness.

For a moment, I felt like I was falling backwards, as if I were in a dream.

I just let go, trying to escape this nightmare in any possible way I could.

I saw a bright light in my mind's eye and started to move toward it.

"I SAID, ARE YOU A SMOKER," her voice snarled, snapping me from my mental departure. "And don't you even try to fall asleep!"

BRANDY BOOTH

I opened my eyes to find she'd leaned my chair back and positioned a big round magnifying light directly in my face.

The blood pressure cuff was gone.

In my confusion, I was momentarily disappointed that I wasn't deceased.

"No," I whispered, my throat too dry to make real noise.

"Your blood pressure is high," she reported.

As the room came back into focus, she fished two beige rubber gloves from a box on the counter.

She exhaled forcefully as she stuck her hand in the first glove.

Although it looked like her hand was all the way in, there was still an inch of empty rubber at the end of each portly digit.

She continued to tug at the cuff until it stretched past her elbow.

BANG!

"Cheap-ass gloves," she cursed, as it gave up and split into three pieces.

"Stupid things never fit right," she grumbled under her breath.

She threw the remains in the trash and started over.

This time she stopped pulling before she reached her elbow.

The bubbles at the ends of her fingers mocked her as she pulled out another glove.

The second one fit the same way.

She cursed again as she alternated cramming stocky fingers inside balled-up fists.

With most of the air squeezed out, she decided it was as good as it was going to get.

It didn't take long to figure out why the gloves didn't fit properly.

I sank deep in the chair as ten chubby thumbs crash landed on the side of my swollen face and pawed to find the eyeball hidden inside.

"Look down. Now up," she said.

I did everything in my power not to look directly at her as her face filled the magnifier.

There was no question that Nurse Edith could grow a better mustache than I could.

She pursed her lips as the surplus rubber kept getting in the way.

Her mouth opened a little wider, exposing uneven green teeth and reddish-white gums.

Each time she folded and pinned the excess finger rubber against my face, a new offender popped up.

And every time it happened, she mashed her digits harder into my injury.

This painful game of whack-a-mole went on for a couple minutes until I let out a squeak and tried to wriggle away.

She lifted her leg and put a knee in my stomach.

"Hold still," the crabby nurse demanded.

Fight or flight was starting to kick in, and I put both hands on her side and pushed, but her torso was like a side of beef, and I didn't move her at all.

She must have known I was close to my breaking point because she removed her knee and stood up.

"I can't find anything. Maybe some numbing solution will keep you from squirming," she decided.

She left the room for a couple minutes and I closed my eyes to pray.

When she re-entered the room, it didn't occur to me that she was on the wrong side until it was too late.

She pried my good eye open and filled it with numbing solution.

"That's the wrong eye," I uttered.

It burned a little, but I didn't care. I could use as much numbing as I could get.

She grunted and circled to the other side.

I cringed as she pried my sore peeper open and squeezed it full of liquid fire.

I blew all the air out of my lungs and tried to wipe it with my sleeve, but she grabbed my arm.

"I know it burns, but you have to let it work."

DID YOU GET ONE OF THESE YET TODAY?

I wondered if I'd actually heard a smidge of compassion in her voice, but quickly dismissed the idea.

As the drops started to take effect, I felt a flicker of hope deep down inside.

"Soon this might all be a bad memory," I thought.

As she reached for my face again, a chunk of fuzz landed under my nose.

I felt a tickle and closed my mouth to keep from eating the unknown object.

As I did, I must have inhaled because the little ball of fur went right up my nose.

To this day, I know it was cat hair.

And to this day, I'm deathly allergic to cats.

The sneeze that came out of nowhere drove my eye into Nurse Edith's hand as I sprayed the magnifier – and Nurse Edith – with spit.

I'll spare you the details of what came out my nose, but it required more than one tissue to clean up.

Surprisingly, she never said a word.

When the mess was cleaned up, she dug in my eye for a few more minutes and admitted she couldn't find anything stuck in it.

"I'm going to try some yellow dye," she announced as she left the room again.

BRANDY BOOTH

I turned my head toward the door as she came back in, making sure she returned to the right side.

She uncapped the bottle, pried my bad eye open, and shot a stream of pee-colored liquid across the bridge of my nose and into my good eye.

She never stopped squirting as she filled the bad eye.

By this point, I didn't care.

The pain had eased because of the numbing solution, and she didn't have to squash me to get me to sit still.

After five more minutes of looking through the magnifier, she gave up.

"The doctor will be here in 45 minutes. You'll have to wait for him."

I breathed a sigh of relief that my encounter with Nurse Edith was coming to an end.

I sat back in the chair and closed my eyes.

"Oh no you don't," she exclaimed. "You're not sleeping in here!"

She left the room and returned with a magazine in her hand.

She threw it in my lap and threatened, "I better not catch you sleeping!"

I did the best I could to pretend I could see the pages with yellow dye running out of my numb eyes.

When the doctor came in, he immediately sent me to an eye specialist to have the rust ring ground from my eyeball.

I never saw Nurse Edith again.

INDUSTRIAL DAY SPA

Biff Buffman was on his way to a meeting in the front office when he walked past the fenced-in area where the millwrights rebuilt gearboxes.

"Aarrgghh!" came a scream from inside the little crib.

Biff paused to listen.

This time he heard laughter.

He took two more steps, and another blood-curdling scream caused him to change direction and walk straight into the crib.

As he cleared the weld curtain, the first thing he saw was Brad Porter bent over the work bench in his underwear and boots.

Wide patches of hair were missing from his back, and little drops of blood were speckled throughout the red patches.

Standing behind him with his back to the door was Tim Shefler.

Shef was holding a big strip of hairy duct tape in his hand, laughing uncontrollably.

"What the..." Biff stammered.

Shef whirled around and squealed with joy when he saw Buffy.

He was thankful that someone else would get to witness this, even if it meant getting into trouble.

"It's not his fault," Brad stammered.

"Can you put some clothes on?" asked Biff.

Shef had tears running down his face as he held up the nasty strip of duct tape and waved it in Biff's direction.

"Come try this. It's a lot of fun," Shef giggled.

"What are you guys doing?" Biff asked, still not sure he wanted the answer.

"Brad's got a high school reunion this weekend, and the people running it rented a block of rooms next to a pool with a hot tub and a tiki bar," Shef explained.

"Brad's worried about his hairy back, so we're taking care of that right now."

"Are you in or out, Buffy?" Shef asked, as he ripped off a fresh chunk of tape.

Biff backed out the door and headed for his meeting.

His pace quickened as Brad let out a half-hearted scream.

"Another fight for another day," Biff thought.

HOW TO STOP A CHOP

In some plants, bullies from one trade liked to pick on the apprentices, no matter if they were from the same trade or not.

DID YOU GET ONE OF THESE YET TODAY?

Steve Huffman was this sort of bully.

A tinsmith by trade (a pretty good one), Steve picked on those around him relentlessly.

He had a special sort of affinity for millwright apprentices, playing as many dirty tricks on them as he could fit into a twelve-hour shift.

"He's going to karate chop your pencils," Jake Sample told me. "He told the guy he's working with that there was only one apprentice left he hadn't gotten yet."

"He broke mine yesterday," he continued. "I was by my toolbox trying to figure out a materials list for the job we're on, and he walked up and chopped my silver pencil in half."

Millwrights typically carry a number two pencil and a silver steel marking pencil on clips in their breast pocket.

Huffman regularly broke new apprentice's pencils when they were on the job together for the first time.

I was being sent out to his job after lunch.

I stared at Jake's broken pencil lying on the bench.

And then I had an idea.

I ate a quick sandwich and headed to the machine repair area to see if they had some metal tubing.

I found one that looked right and stuck my pencil in just to be sure.

The thick metal tubing was exactly the right diameter.

I took it to the cut-off wheel, sanded the ends, and slipped the new protective covers into place.

It seemed a little bulkier, but you couldn't see the hidden reinforcement.

When I showed up on the job a few minutes after lunch, Steve was already clamping pieces together.

Things were pretty quiet as we assembled the new conveyor system.

And then it was time for me to weld some brackets in place.

I saw Steve eyeing me up as I put my welding hood on and pulled the thick leather gloves up my arms.

His best opportunity to strike would be when I had my hood down to weld.

I dropped my hood, stretched out my arm, and got ready to start my arc.

I waited a second or two for the blow that never came, but then I heard my boss talking to another person behind me.

Steve was a dumbass, but he wasn't stupid enough to strike when the boss was standing right there.

A few minutes went by, and I moved through the first welds fairly quickly.

I'd just finished one of the main supports and was reaching to lift my helmet when Steve launched his ill-fated assault.

The force of the blow to my chest knocked me off balance, but it didn't hurt too bad.

But Steve didn't get off so easy.

One of the guys who watched it happen said he'd put everything he had into that side-arm chop.

Now he was hopping around in a circle, howling in pain, and holding his hand.

When he finally stood upright, I snatched the pencils out of his pocket and tossed them in the air above his head, where he bobbled them before they hit the floor.

THE WEENIE ROAST

Every welder has a story of a molten chunk of slag burning a hole into the top of their foot, next to their belly button, or – heaven forbid - someplace even worse.

Many have scars they can show you.

Some have scars they can't.

_____

Chester Putz was having a good day.

He'd learned to weld ductwork that morning and had fallen in love with MIG welding right away.

Shef had watched him work for a while, but Chester's welds were solid, so he'd gone back to helping Brad Porter roll and tack the pieces to build new elbows.

Chester smiled as he dropped his hood.

This was way better than the welding he'd done at school.

There were no long beads in the classroom, only short test passes and small projects.

Welding these six-foot diameter sections of ductwork was a completely different animal altogether.

If you played your cards right, you could weld for ten minutes straight and never stop.

Chester looked across the shop at the piles of ductwork pieces yet to be welded together.

"I could weld for weeks and still not finish all this," he thought.

He started whistling as he began a new pass.

One of the old welders had taught him to whistle a tune to keep in-time as he stitched steel together with fire and wire.

He'd burned through every Johnny Cash song he knew and had discovered that some were too slow to weld to.

He planned to try some ZZ Top on his next pass.

"Weld the elbow on the table," Shef directed. "Once that's done, we can cut it loose and free up space to build another piece."

Chester looked at the huge round elbow that seemed to sprout from the big metal table.

They'd tacked it together earlier in the week and left it there for show.

This macaroni-shaped giant was one cool looking piece of sheet metal.

Chester had been eyeing it up for the past couple of days, and Shef knew he'd been itching to weld it.

"Do a good job on that one. It hangs closest to the aisle where everyone will see it." Shef coached.

Chester didn't need to be told to do a good job on this big beauty.

He was focused, plus if he got off track a little bit, he had a grinder to fix it.

Chester clamped on the ground and hung the MIG gun over the hook on the side of the table.

He pulled the little set of steps around to the side, grabbed his hood and gloves, and climbed up on the table.

It didn't take him long to drop his hood and get going.

As he did, Tim and Brad continued to roll and tack new pieces together on the next table.

"He's getting the hang of it," Brad said to Tim.

"Yeah, but don't tell him. It goes straight to his head," Tim replied.

They both looked over at their newest apprentice.

Chester was stretched out on his tiptoes against the big elbow trying to reach the highest point he could weld.

As the MIG gun continued to hum and crackle, a small river of red slag slipped off the top of the elbow and disappeared into his coveralls.

His whistling sputtered, then slowed to a stop as his hips began to dance around.

Without warning, he jerked his body to the left, let go of the MIG gun, and grabbed the edge of the big piece to keep himself from falling off the table.

The MIG gun slid down the side of the big pipe as he reached down to pull his coveralls away from his body, shaking them while kicking his right leg.

"GGaahh!!!" he howled, as his gloves and hood went flying in all different directions.

He leapt off the table and bounced on the balls of his feet a few times before skidding to a stop with his hands on his knees, drawing labored breaths through clenched teeth.

"Are you alright?" Brad asked, as Chester hissed and tried not to pass out.

Chester didn't give an answer as his eyes filled with water.

He looked up at Shef, who repeated Brad's question.

Chester shook his head from side to side and squeaked, "I need to go to the locker room for a minute."

And he dashed up the stairs.

About five minutes later, Chester came back down with a serious look on his face.

"I don't know what to do," he said.

"I burnt the head of my dick pretty badly. Can you guys see what you think?"

"That's above my pay grade," Shef declined, as he held up his hand.

"I'm NOT looking at it, either!" Brad said quickly.

"I think I'm going to have to go to medical," Chester mumbled. "The burn is as big as a dime."

"So pretty much the whole thing," Shef giggled.

"Guys! This is serious! I don't know what to do!" Chester whined.

"Well, you don't want it to get infected and fall off," Brad joked.

"Want us to take you up there?" Shef asked with a grin.

"No. Showing this to Megan will be hard enough without you two clowns teasing me," he groaned.

Just then, the boss pulled up on his three-wheeled cart.

"The apprentice has something he wants to show you," Brad said, as he pointed at Chester with his thumb.

"What's up?" the supervisor asked, as he leaned around to see.

"Can you run me up to the nurse?" Chester asked.

"He's got a tiny boo-boo," Shef laughed, as he squinted and pinched his fingers together.

195

Chester hunched over on the back seat as the two rode away.

"Oh, to be a fly on the wall in medical today... Wouldn't that be great?" Shef exclaimed.

"Poor Megan doesn't know it yet, but there's a little fun headed her way..."

A few weeks later, maintenance gathered for their health and safety meeting when the past month's recordables were brought up.

"We had one injury last month," the boss said, as he tried to quickly move on to the next item on the agenda.

"Wait! What happened?" Shef asked.

The boss hung his head and looked at the floor. He knew what was coming.

"We just want to understand what happened, so we know how to keep ourselves safe," Brad added.

"I mean - isn't the reason we have these meetings and go over this stuff so we can learn from it and not do it again?" Shef volleyed.

"Screw you guys!" Chester busted in, with a wide-eyed laugh. "I'm DEFINITELY not doing THAT again!"

Shef tossed something in Chester's lap and told him to try it on for size.

It turned out to be a pinky-finger cut off from a woman's welding glove.

"If it's too big, use a rubber band to hold it in place," Brad tortured.

It took a long time for Chester to live that one down.

Chapter Seven

Horseplay

horse-play *noun* – rough, boisterous play.

The first time I read Shop Rule 13: "No Horseplay", I didn't know what it meant.

I've gained a lot of knowledge and experience since then.

And I can tell you from both observation and participation:

Of all the shop rules ever written - this one is the most fun to break.

BACK AT 'YA!

Andy Carrier was tired of getting wet.

He'd rotated a few times and had taken a single hit at the end of every rotation, but one person in this plant had started throwing water nearly a week early.

The thing was – this water thrower wasn't even someone who should have been throwing water at Andy at all.

Chester Putz had nearly gotten Andy wet twice with the hose that hung on the column near the tool crib.

Although apprentices didn't typically throw water at other apprentices, Chester didn't care about rules and thought it would be a fun thing to do.

Now Andy couldn't even go to the crib without Chester trying to spray him.

With two more days left to go, Andy would just have to avoid that area.

"Did he try to shoot you with that hose too?" Buckshot Flanerty asked Andy.

"Yes, twice already this week," he groaned.

"He's been spraying all the other apprentices, too, even mine," Buckshot said, as he shook his head.

"That makes me mad, because MY apprentice is MINE to get wet."

Andy liked the tone of Buckshot's voice.

This man was legend throughout the plants for being the best water thrower to ever strap on a pair of work boots.

From what Andy could hear, it sounded like Chester was about to get what he deserved, and maybe even a little extra.

"A Blowback Nozzle," Buckshot said out of the blue.

"A what?" Andy asked.

"A Blowback Nozzle is when you plug weld the end of the hose nozzle and drill a diagonal hole that points back at the person holding the hose," Buckshot explained.

"The best ones have a chunk of tubing tacked inside the diagonal hole to make a good stream. That's what we need here," he said.

"When Putz goes to shoot you from the corner by the crib, he'll get a face full of water."

"What do you mean, shoot ME?" Andy chirped. "My plan is just to stay the hell away from him."

"Well, that's why I came to see you. I would have used my own apprentice as bait, but I slipped up and told Chester I was going to slap him upside the head with a pipe wrench if he got my apprentice wet again."

"I want to get him, and I need your help to do it."

"Buckshot looked Andy in the eye, and he instantly knew there was no way he'd get away with refusing.

Besides, Buckshot's bad side wasn't a dry place to be.

Andy agreed to be the bait and asked what he needed to do.

"Just pull up to that corner and sit until he tries to shoot you with the hose that hangs on that column. Be there at 7:50 am tomorrow just before the eight o'clock huddle. I'll have the trap set and ready to go," Buckshot laughed.

"Wait, what if he tries to shoot someone else with it before I come along? And how is he not going to see a big hole drilled in the top of the nozzle?" Andy inquired.

"If he shoots someone else, I guess you're off the hook, so to speak," Buckshot reasoned.

"And I always put a big dab of grease in the hole that's the same color as the pipe, and I level it off so it blends in. He'll never see it."

Andy thought about it some more and reluctantly agreed.

Even if Chester got him wet, the others might take that as Andy's last day hit and let him off.

Truth be told, there weren't many things Andy Carrier hated more than getting wet.

At 7:49 the next morning, Andy drove down the back aisle toward the crib.

Chester saw him coming and took off running for his ambush spot.

As Andy slowly rounded the corner, Chester sprang from behind the column, extended his arms, and held the hose straight out in front of him.

"Happy last day in the plant, you lowlife apprentice!" Chester yelled.

Andy slammed on the brakes, and Chester cranked the water valve open.

The instant he did, a high-pressure stream of water hit him squarely between the eyes, peeling the glasses off his face and blowing his hair back.

Chester didn't seem to comprehend what was happening for a moment, cocking his head to the side and trying to see what obstructed the end of the wand with the water still spraying.

Andy started driving again and was right beside him when Chester finally thought to turn the valve off.

A thick dab of grease hung from Chester's forehead, and his eyes were out of focus from the high-pressure beating they'd taken, but Chester wasn't giving up yet.

As Andy drove past, Chester tried turning the hose back on and holding it in a way where the stream would hit Andy, but he only succeeded in getting himself even wetter.

Andy looked back to make sure Chester wasn't chasing him as he rounded the corner.

When he turned back around, he had to slam on the brakes to avoid hitting Buckshot, who was standing in the middle of the aisle holding a hose twice the size of the one Chester had tried using on him.

"Your journeymen said it was okay if I handled your last-day hit," he announced.

"Seriously?!?" Andy choked, as his eyes darted for a place to escape. "C'mon, man..."

"No apprentice has left this plant dry since I came here ten years ago. You can't be the one blemish on my record, son."

Andy tried to jump and run, but Buckshot's aim was deadly.

FORGED IN STEEL

"I'll bet nobody reads the receiving slips at all. They're just useless paperwork that gets thrown away without ever being looked at," Brad Porter said.

"You're probably right," said Donnie Tompkins. "I usually just scribble a line across it."

When millwrights unloaded steel trucks, they signed a receiving slip and gave it to their maintenance leader, where (they figured) it probably disappeared into oblivion.

Nobody looked for the slips unless there was a problem with the steel order, but that hardly ever happened.

When it did, they rarely found the slip they were looking for because someone had put it in their pocket or thrown it away by mistake.

"I'm certain nobody ever sees them. I've signed my name as 'Belly Button' several times," Brad giggled. "If nobody's going to see it, I might as well have a laugh."

"We should get everybody doing it," Donnie said.

Brad knew all the other millwrights who unloaded steel and worked in the back yards at all six plants in the division.

In fact, James "Fuzzy" Johnson unloaded the steel trucks at the plant next door, and he was retiring at the end of the month.

"Wouldn't it be great if the millwrights across the division all signed 'Fuzzy Johnson' every time they unloaded a steel truck?" Brad asked Donny.

"We'd probably never get caught, and if we did, what could they say?"

Brad went to see Fuzzy first.

Fuzzy was getting ready to retire, and there wasn't too much that could bother him these days.

He smiled and nodded at their tribute, knowing full well there wasn't anything he could do to stop it.

It took about a week for Brad and Donnie to get all the millwrights on-board with the idea, but they all did.

For the next eight months, millwrights across the division signed "Fuzzy Johnson" every time they unloaded a steel truck.

And then one day, a load of high-priority steel was delivered to the wrong plant.

In trying to track it down, receiving slips from three different plants were scrutinized.

All said they'd been unloaded by this "Fuzzy Johnson" guy who had retired eight months before.

Needless to say, the next maintenance meeting in every plant talked about forgery, horseplay, and the proper way to fill out company paperwork.

THE FAKE PASS

It wasn't easy to know where to go in the Prototype Center.

The place was huge and seemed to be unorganized.

Engineers, students, and customers from all over the world constantly traveled between the plants and prototype.

But once they passed through the staging garage, many didn't know how to locate the proper room where a certain product was being tested, as there were several hundred rooms and test stations.

For years, confused people wandered the halls of this state-of-the-art test facility, searching for the product they were assigned to improve.

In the early days, Brad Porter used to give people bad directions or tell them their destination was in a completely different direction than it was.

But one day, Brad had the idea to make up passes that he could give to people when he sent them on their wild goose chase.

Because Tim Shefler had a computer, printer, and laminator, Brad went to see if he could help create a pass he could give the people wandering about.

Shef loved the idea, and they put their heads together to create a form that would fit their needs.

Eventually, they came up with the "Fake Pass".

BRANDY BOOTH

The Fake Pass was an official-looking form that said "Fake Pass" right at the top, followed by a space for the person's name, their company's name, the date, contact person, product, shoe color, eye color, weight, and two spaces for additional comments.

Once a person had filled it out, they were instructed to give it to security at the end of the long hallway, who would look up their room number and provide them with a map to where they needed to go.

(Security had already been doing this for years.)

Of course, the security guards all thought this was hilarious and played along with the trick as they directed the person to the right room.

They said the men would usually ask why the form wanted to know their shoe color, while the women wanted to know if they really had to include their weight.

Now, if you're thinking this sounds ridiculous and would never work on anyone, consider that many of the people wandering about the Prototype Center looking lost were engineers from our sister plants around the world.

Others were just thankful someone showed up to help when they were lost.

Whatever the case may have been, Brad and Shef knew how to pick the gullible ones.

And for all I know, people might still be using fake passes to find their way around over there to this day.

#1 WELDER

Jerry Shoultes dropped his hood and began to weld the angle iron bracket I'd tacked together.

He immediately stopped his arc, let out a low whistle, set his stinger down, took off his gloves, and removed his welding helmet.

I didn't know why he'd stopped, but I knew something wasn't right.

He set his hood on the table and popped out the clip that holds the glass lens, magnifier, and tinted welding glass sandwiched together in front of his face.

As he separated the tinted lens from the protective glass, a black piece of paper fell out and landed on the table.

I leaned in to see what it was, and it was a cutout of a woman in a sexy pose.

"That's a good one," Jerry said to Brad.

"I thought so," Brad replied. "I saw you could use a new lens, so I grabbed one from the crib when I was there."

"Since yours is already out, here ya go," he grinned.

"Thanks," Jerry said, as he popped in the new lens and went back to welding.

Jerry and Brad had been friends a long time and were both pretty mellow, so Jerry didn't get mad about having a harmless trick played on him every once in a while.

BRANDY BOOTH

Most of the guys were pretty mellow back then.

Burt Labowski, on the other hand, did not appreciate jokes that came at his expense.

He liked to mess with others but had a tendency to go full crybaby when others messed with him.

His clean-shaven face and hard belly made him look like a large, chubby infant when he went on a rant, which was deeply satisfying to those who had to put up with him.

Burt wasn't a bad welder, but he did have a few quirks.

For one, he was picky about how his welding cables were wrapped, as I discovered one day when I'd wrapped them wrong by mistake, (or so he says).

I'd noticed his cables were dirty at the end of our job, so I wiped all the dirt and grease off and coiled them on their hangers so the loops were nice and even.

He took one look at what I'd done, let out a huff, grabbed both coils and threw them on the ground.

"I like my cables wrapped so the wires lay a certain way," he snapped, as he wrapped them almost exactly the same as I'd done.

I kept my distance after that, but we still ended up on the same job from time to time.

One day, Brad Porter and Tim Shefler called Burt out to weld a bracket on the assembly line while the line was down for lunch.

DID YOU GET ONE OF THESE YET TODAY?

When Burt dropped his hood to strike an arc, there was a big black cutout of a middle finger sandwiched between his lenses that completely blocked his view.

He let out a yell, threw down his stinger, crossed over the line, and waddled back to his cart.

"You're the number one welder in my book," Shef laughed.

Burt threw his welding hood down on the front seat and walked around the back of the cart to grab the old junk hood that always hung on the side of the cart.

He crossed back over the line, put his gloves and hood back on, and crouched into position to start his arc once more.

This time, he yelled even louder and threw his slag hammer as the bright light revealed a big penis cutout that completely obstructed his view.

"You assholes keep clowning around and I'm never welding your shit again!!" he threatened.

"Settle down, Burt," Shef said. "A good welder wouldn't let a little thing like not being able to see stop him from burning rod."

Burt wheezed as he climbed back over the line and threw the old hood in the box on the back of the cart.

He grabbed his other hood, snapped the lens out, crumpled the piece of paper up, and snapped the lenses back into place.

"Now stop screwing around!" he growled.

He was almost finished welding when the horn blew for the line to start back up.

The supervisor came running up wanting to know why the job hadn't been finished in time.

Brad and Shef both told him to ask the number one welder...

BRAKE CHECK

"The new flatbed carts suck!" Chester Putz complained.

The group of trades around the break table didn't look up when Chester began to complain.

Eye contact seemed to egg him on.

"They only go eight miles an hour, and the brake engages every time you let off the gas. You can't even coast to a stop on those stupid things. I tried to sneak up on the fitters earlier, but the engine brake lets 'em know you're coming from a mile away!"

"Turn the key off before you let off the gas," Lisa Swift shrugged. "Once the power is cut, the cart will free-wheel and the brake motor won't engage."

"Good to know!" Chester winked. "In fact, I'm going to try it right now. Rocky needs a ride back from the other end of the plant."

As Chester hopped on his cart and rode away, Brad told Lisa, "You know, we had carts at my old plant that used to automatically set the parking brake if they lost power. It was a built-in safety feature."

"Yup," Lisa nodded. "These work the same way."

"You told Chester the brake *wouldn't* engage if the power was cut," Brad said, grinning from ear to ear.

"Yep, that IS what I told Chester," Lisa smirked, as she raised her eyebrows and sipped her iced tea.

The group shifted in their seats as Chester came down the aisle full speed with Rocky in the passenger seat.

Rocky was writing something on his clipboard when Chester reached down and hit the key next to the tool crib.

Without warning, the rear wheels locked up, causing the cart to nosedive before it started bucking wildly and skidded out of control.

Rocky let go of his clipboard and tried grabbing for the metal handle in front of him.

He got it on the third try, but not before slamming his knee and elbow against the dash.

Tools, rags, and metal bread pans came slamming forward, raining nuts, bolts, and washers off the sides like candy in a parade.

Chester had tried to turn the key back on, but the sudden stop rolled him over the front and left him hanging by the steering wheel.

When the flatbed finally came to rest against a building column, Rocky hobbled off and yelled, "What the hell did you do, you dumbass apprentice?"

Although Rocky hadn't been paying attention when Chester turned the key off, he was one hundred percent certain that Chester had done *something* to cause what happened.

"What did you do, pull the e-brake?! I'm never riding with you again, you jackass."

Lisa got up from the table and walked away down the aisle.

She'd owed Chester some lumps for picking on her at welding school, but this didn't even begin to pay him back all the way.

"It's a decent start," she thought.

THE RUDE AWAKENING

John Stone was going through a rough patch.

He had a new baby at home, a sick wife, and two other kids with busy school schedules.

One morning, he walked into the shop looking like he hadn't slept for a week.

"Rough night?" asked Charlie Sagebrush.

"It's incredible how much my wife gets done during a normal day around there," John yawned.

"She tried to help with the baby last night, but he just didn't want to go to sleep."

"Well, the other guys and I can handle the job this morning if you want to hang around, clean up the shop, and rest up until we need you," Charlie informed.

DID YOU GET ONE OF THESE YET TODAY?

"I'm good," John replied. "I can carry my own weight."

"No, stay here," Charlie said. "The apprentice is going to run the crane today for the first pick. It's time he got used to driving the overhead. We'll be back before lunch."

"Well, I appreciate it. I have to pick the kids up after work, get them something to eat, and have them to volleyball practice by four," John muttered.

He did some cleaning in the shop while the rest of the crew went to the job.

When they came back for lunch, John wasn't there.

One of the apprentices heard snoring coming from the back room and found him sound asleep in the chair behind the leaf brake.

He was sleeping so hard that the drool hanging from the corner of his mouth nearly reached his shoulder.

"He's really out," Charlie told the crew. "Let's have some fun!"

"When you're done eating lunch, grab your lunch buckets and jackets and lock up your toolboxes. Then head out the side door and hang out at the picnic tables until I come get you."

They did as they were told, and Charlie went around to the three clocks in the department and set them all to 3:25.

(Day shift ended at 2:30 pm.)

When everybody was in place, Sagebrush switched off the lights, slammed the heavy door, and hid in the broom closet in the corner to watch.

He heard a noise from the back room like a chair tipped over, and John came running out to look at the clocks above the workstations.

"NO! NO! NO!" He cried. "It can't be almost 3:30!"

He grabbed his coat and lunch box and ran out the door toward the front of the plant.

Fifteen minutes later, he came strolling back into the department where the crew had their tools back out and were getting ready to go back out on the job.

"You ready to go to work yet?" Sagebrush asked.

"That was a really good one," John said as he shook his head.

"I almost made it out the turnstile, but the parking lot didn't look right to me for an hour after shift change."

"Then I looked up at the time clock, and it said 12:03, and it still didn't dawn on me right away. I had to stand there and think for a minute, then the plant secretary came back with her salad from down the road, and it hit me."

THAT'S A WRAP!

When the whistle went off at nine and one, Ritchie Robinson would run for the little break room to get the good bench in front of the air conditioner.

Nobody had beaten him to it yet.

He literally ran.

DID YOU GET ONE OF THESE YET TODAY?

Since the day after he'd come to this crappy department four weeks ago, this was HIS spot during break.

It didn't matter if it had been someone else's spot before he'd arrived.

"First come, first served," he'd yawn, as the displaced workers protested.

And they had good reason to be angry.

You see, Richie wouldn't simply take up one seat in the tiny room that only fit eight people.

He'd take his boots off, pull his hat down, and stretch out the length of the bench with his arms and legs crossed, taking up *three* spots.

Two weeks after he'd started this nonsense, Frankie Ford and Randy "Tubby" Rhineheart had literally picked him up and thrown him and his stinky feet off the bench, but Richie ran straight to labor relations.

The labor rep agreed it wasn't right that Richie had transferred into their department and claimed the three best spots when there weren't enough to go around, but they couldn't have their employees resorting to physical force, either.

"Try to put up with him until his paperwork goes through," the labor rep said. "As soon as he got to your department, he realized it wasn't where he wanted to be, and he transferred again. It should only be another week or two."

"You're not even going to tell him to only take up one spot?" Randy asked in disbelief.

The labor rep looked down and they both knew it wasn't going to be addressed.

"Well, if he keeps up the way he's going, I'll see you back here soon," Frankie snorted.

"Me too. And look into where they're at on getting us a break area big enough to fit the whole team," Randy added.

"Make it big enough so we can all lay down," Frankie smirked.

Frankie and Randy shook their heads as they walked back to their department.

This wasn't right.

Richie wasn't high on the seniority list.

He barely had enough whiskers to hold days, let alone to waltz in and take their department over.

This wasn't right at all.

The older women at the far end of the line had stopped coming to the break area because they knew they'd never get a seat by the time they walked there.

Their only option was to sit on the hard metal benches along the wall or at the rickety picnic tables outside the back door.

The August heat made it unbearable in both places, but there was no other option.

"Two more weeks? It's just not right," Tubby said to Frankie as they stood outside the break room.

Frankie shook his head in disgust.

"Look at him lying there like it's his own personal flophouse and he's top dog."

This wasn't right at all.

Two weeks went by and there was no word on Richie's transfer or their new break area.

"Looks like we're going to have to help the process along," Frankie shrugged, as he smacked the huge zip ties together in his hand.

"Today's as good a day as any," Randy said, as he headed to the end of the line where the shrink wrap machine sat.

He opened the little cabinet next to it and took out two hand-held shrink wrap dispensers.

When they got to the break area, Richie was in his usual spot with his boots off, his legs crossed, and his hat pulled over his face.

Two guys got up from their seats and slid out the door when they saw what was about to go down, but the other four just sat there.

As Frankie and Randy knelt on either side of the bench and passed the ends of the big zip ties underneath, Richie reached up to rub his nose, almost touching Frankie's arm.

When he put his arm back down, they nodded at each other and jerked the ends of the big zip ties all at once, cinching one just above Richie's kneecaps and another around his arms and torso just above his elbows.

217

Richie's eyes popped open, and he got one arm free before Randy grabbed it and pushed it back against his side.

As Frankie started to shrink wrap his arms, Richie let out a yell, but nobody here was going to help him.

These people had been smelling his stinky feet every day for the last month.

No, they weren't going to help him, and the boss couldn't hear him, either.

He let out another scream, and Frankie ripped off his left sock and shoved it in his mouth.

"I'll put 'em both in there and tape your mouth shut," Frankie growled.

Richie tried to wiggle his way off the side of the bench, but Frankie leaned against him and said, "If you don't think we'll leave you hanging off the bottom of this bench, you don't understand what's happening here. It might be better to stay where you're at."

Richie stopped struggling after the first layer of shrink wrap was on.

He pushed his chest and belly out so the wrap wouldn't suffocate him, and they put on two more layers for good measure.

All but one person had left the break area by the time they were done, but break wasn't even half over.

Frankie set Richie's hat back over his face and picked up his boots.

These things stink," Frankie winced, as he set them on Richie's chest.

When the whistle blew after break, the "line down" music immediately started to play.

After about two minutes, the boss showed up looking for Richie, but nobody had seen him.

The coordinator was instructed to fill in on Richie's job, and the line began to run.

It didn't take long for the boss to discover Richie shrink wrapped to the bench.

After about fifteen minutes, they walked out together and headed up front.

Frankie figured he was getting called for a disciplinary interview when the boss showed up nearly an hour later, but he calmly said, "Richie's transfer came through today. He's gone on Monday and isn't working the weekend."

"Oh, and they found a bigger break area with an air conditioner in both ends. They'll be installing it next weekend."

He paused and looked at the ground.

Frankie waited for what he knew was still coming.

"They wanted me to write you two up for horseplay and misuse of company property," he added.

"But they told me to ask for witnesses, and nobody came forward, so it's your word against his."

"I'm innocent," Frankie confessed.

"No doubt," his boss replied.

FINAL BOX CHECK

When skilled tradespeople retire, they're allowed to take their toolbox with them after it's been inspected for company property.

There are usually four people at the toolbox inspection: the employee, his supervisor, his committeeman, and a security guard to tag and seal the box shut after it's been approved.

But when Fred Brown retired, there were more than twenty people standing around the area where his box was to be inspected, including a dozen of his fellow tool and die makers.

I could tell something was up by the crazy energy in the air.

Fred was one of the good guys who everyone liked.

He planned on opening a barber shop after he retired because he loved telling stories that made people laugh.

(On this day, he'd end up with a pretty good one to add to his collection!)

It all started when Fred's boss (Jack Lang) called me to come watch Fred's box inspection.

When boxes are inspected, the employee pulls out each drawer one-by-one and the boss looks at the contents and either says yes or pulls out a particular tool and decides whether it stays in the plant or goes home with him.

DID YOU GET ONE OF THESE YET TODAY?

As a committeeman, it was my job to convince the boss to leave all the tools in the employee's box.

When Fred pulled out the top drawer, everything looked normal.

But just as he went to close it, Jack Lang reached in and grabbed a pencil that had a funny-looking eraser on the end that turned out to be a miniature penis.

Fred snatched it from his hand and examined it closer.

He turned to the group of pranksters leaning on their boxes.

Everyone thought he was going to say something, but he just set the pencil on the box and opened the second drawer.

"WHAT THE!?!?" he stammered.

"Jesus, Fred," Jack snickered. "Isn't your wife a few sizes smaller than this?"

Jack fished out a pair of granny panties big enough to fit a grizzly.

"Is there something we should know, Fred? Do these fit you?"

"You guys..." Fred chuckled and tried to hide his face.

One of his fellow toolmakers stepped out with a camera.

"Hold them up high, Fred," another poked.

(That photo is probably on the wall in Fred's barber shop.)

By the time they were through, they found a junior barbershop kit, a Willy Warmer, five penis-shaped suckers, fake poop, a picture of Jack Lang's wife (stolen off his desk the week before), and an all-in-one drag queen costume.

Fred's face was bright red from laughing so hard at the sendoff he received at the end of his automotive career.

Mine was too, because I like funny things.

Want More?

If you've enjoyed these stories and want more, go to www.autoworkertales.com and download a free copy of "Autoworker Tales: Straight from the Factory."

Inside, you'll find seven more stories from the <u>Autoworker Tales</u> collection, including:

1. A Template for Mischief

2. The Sleepy Professor

3. Look! Under There!

4. A Picture is Worth a Thousand Words

5. Lemon Appeal

6. Mum's the Word

7. Switch!

Share the Laughs

• • • ● ● ● • ● • • •

When a story makes you think of a friend, coworker, or family member, it's an opportunity to share a laugh.

In today's world, we can use as many of those as we can get.

"Did You Get One of THESE Yet Today" makes a great gift idea for that special person who:

- Spent time in or around the automotive industry.

- Retired from an industrial or repetitious job.

- Enjoys pranks and funny situations.

- Might enjoy receiving a book that pops the question.

- Likes funny things.

There's gold in those stories that always seem to come up between old friends.

Having new ones to share adds fuel to those good times.

Did You Get One of THESE Yet Today is perfect for the following occasions, including:

- Retirements

- Birthdays

- Mother's / Father's Day

- Christmas

- Celebrating a new apprenticeship or journeying out

- Get well soon

- Going away

- Or just an unexpected hello

<u>Sneak Attack!</u>

Imagine the look on that special person's face when they open the gift that subtly pops the question!

Thanks for Reading!

I appreciate the opportunity to share these stories with you!

101 Ways to Pop the Question

1. **The Original** – "Excuse me Sir / Ma'am. Did You Get One of THESE Yet Today?"

2. **"You Dropped This"** – Bend over like you're picking something up and BAM.

3. **Simple Subtraction** – "Do you know what 67 - 66 is?" Show them the answer as you say it.

4. **Happy New Year!** - "It's 1 - 1!" (Use both hands.)

5. **The Volume Knob** - "Hey, can you hear this, or do you need me to turn it up? (Start with your bird on its side and rotate it as you slowly say the word "up.")

6. **The Fake Toss** - Pretend like you're quick-tossing something at them and end up in the single digit salute. Bonus points if you get them to flinch.

7. **Pixie Dust** - Reach in your breast pocket like you're grabbing a pinch of dust and sprinkle it on your fist, causing something magical to appear.

8. **The Screw-On** - Pull a fist out of one pocket and fish around in the other, bringing a fist out and acting like you're screwing a finger in place as you sneak your finger inside. Viola!

9. **The Fishing Pole** - Hold one fist up with your knuckles facing the ceiling. With the other hand, act like you're reeling a fishing pole as your finger cranks up into position.

10. **The Cleanup** - Holding one hand flat like a board, grab a rag and start wiping it until you clean it into something useful.

11. **"What's that Behind Your Ear?"** - Hint: it's not a quarter...

12. **The King Cobra** - Pretend you're playing a flute with one hand as your other hand snakes back and forth until it stands fully erect.

13. **The Fairy Godmother** - Point your wand at your fist and say "Bibbity bobbity boo!"

14. **Mind Control** - Put one hand against your head and hold the other in a fist in front of you. Squint like

you're lifting a mental boulder as your finger slowly unfolds.

15. **The Card Trick** - Hold your fist up and fan the other hand over the top as if you were spreading a deck of cards, revealing your ace in the hole.

16. **The Scarface** - "Say hello to my little friend..."

17. **Pay it Forward** - "Someone gave me one of THESE, so now I'm gifting it to you. Make sure to pass it along..."

18. **The Show-Off** - "Hey! Check out how long my finger is!"

19. **The Ouchie** - If you've injured the proper finger (or you can use a band-aid as a prop.) "See! I got an ouchie!"

20. **Examine THIS** - "If you look real close, you can see a faint scar..."

21. **The Whirlybird** - Spin your arm in a circle until your little birdie pops out.

22. **The Major League Pitcher** - Wind up and let 'er fly!

23. **The Talk Show Host** – "YOU win a prize, and YOU win a prize. Hell, EVERYONE gets a prize..."

24. **Junk in the Trunk** - Reach behind you and...well... Pull one out your backside.

25. **The Tour Guide** - "If you look over there, you'll see... Now direct your attention to this..."

26. **The Air Pump** - Squeeze your forearm like the ball on a blood pressure cuff until it builds enough pressure to pop the question.

27. **The Misplaced Messenger** - Pat yourself down and fish through your pockets until you find what you're looking for. "Oh, here it is!"

28. **Jack-in-the-Box** - Get a box. You know the rest.

29. **Last Man Standing** - Make a finger gun to shoot the non-middle fingers off the other hand while making a "pew-pew" sound.

30. **The Helping Hand** - With your arm hanging limply by your side, grab it, spin it upright, and fold the outside fingers down one-by-one.

31. **The Fake Injury** - Say "Ow, I got a cramp in my finger." Then wince like it's pulling itself upward against your will.

32. **Rock. Paper. Finger.** - Self-explanatory.

33. **Give the Date** - When someone asks the date, show them as you say it. Works with the first, second, eleventh, and twenty-second.

34. **Thumb Jack** - While giving the thumbs-up, jack your thumb up and down like you're raising a car.

35. **Balloon Finger** - Blow on your thumb like you're blowing up a balloon. Once they've seen it, let go and make a show of the air coming out.

36. **Stuck Shut** - Hold your fist up like you're trying to give the finger. Slap the side a couple times until it unjams and your boy makes an appearance.

37. **The Tin Man** – Oil your joints with a pretend can, set it down, and make creaking sounds as you bend each finger back and forth. A little more oil, then show 'em how nice the middle one works.

38. **The Magician** - Throw a rag over your fist and wave your fingers while saying your favorite magic words. Pull the rag off, and there you have it.

39. **The Second Choice** - Make a fist with one hand and use the other to unfold the wrong finger. Fold it back down and get it right.

40. **The Lumberjack** - Making chainsaw noises, use your pointer finger as a little saw to cut all but the longest finger off the other hand.

41. **Pull My Finger** - Act like you're pulling your fingers off and tossing them aside until there's only one left.

42. **The Wrist Button** - Poke your pointer finger into the middle of your wrist and pop your weasel every time it makes contact.

43. **Lost and Found** - "Hey, if anyone turns any of THESE in, I lost a whole satchel full."

44. **Autoworker Pie** - "This ONE time...at band camp..."

45. **The Visual Storyteller** - "It was ONE year ago today..."

46. **The Sneak Attack** - Start by giving a thumbs-up, then slowly extend your finger as you rotate it up with a grin.

47. **Strike!** – Pretend you're bowling. Follow through with the bird.

48. **One-a-Day** - "THESE are like vitamins. If you don't get at least one, your day just isn't the same..."

49. **Doctor's Orders** - "Take two of THESE and call me in the morning."

50. **The Forward-Facing Compliment** - "You're #1 in my book!"

51. **The Wacky Wallcrawler** - But instead of shooting a web...

52. **Clear for Takeoff** – "You DON'T need a pilot's license to fly one of THESE..."

53. **The Trusted Friend** - "Here, keep this safe for me..."

54. **The Dead Insect** - Pretend like there's an insect flying around your head. Snatch at the air and slowly open your hand to reveal...

55. **The Lollipop** - Pretend to lick your fist until your finger stands up. (Also known as "Cat Paw" or "Ice Cream Cone.")

56. **Fresh is Better** – "It's best to give and receive them regularly. Keeps 'em fresh..."

57. **The Turn Signal** - With your fist on its side. flip your

finger open and closed to indicate which direction you'll be turning.

58. **The Sobriety Check** - Act like you're walking a heel-to-toe line while trying to touch your nose with your eyes closed using your middle fingers.

59. **One in the Boot** - If your regular shooter runs out of lead, kneel down and grab your spare. Bang! Bang!

60. **The Optometrist** - "How many fingers am I holding up?" (Hint: the answer is ALWAYS one.)

61. **The Lone Diner** - "Table for ONE please..."

62. **Shush the f*ck up!** - Sends a stronger message than putting your pointer finger up to your lips.

63. **The Drummer** - Middle fingers are more entertaining than air drumsticks.

64. **The Head Rub** - Use both hands to rub the back of your head. Slowly slide them forward and do a smooth transition into a double-fisted salute.

65. **Catch a Tiger** - Say "eenie, meanie, miney, MOE..." as you fold the lesser fingers down one at a time.

66. **The Sundial** - Hold your finger high in the air while using the other hand as a visor. Squint at the sun, look down at your shadow, and announce, "It's 2:37."

67. **Goalposts** - Get between THESE babies, score 3 points!

68. **Fists of Fury** - Drop back into your best fighting stance, let out a long "WWwwooohhhh!!" and slowly extend your finger.

69. **The Marshaller** - You've seen the guy on the tarmac telling planes where to go. Instead of those orange things, direct traffic with what you were born with.

70. **No Time to Talk** - If you walk past a doorway and notice someone inside as you pass, lean forward and swing your greeting into the opening behind you, but keep going.

71. **The Gunfighter** - Walk ten paces, turn, and shoot.

72. **The Mime Artist** - With your legs to your sides, place your hands flat on the pretend glass in front of you. Move your head over and roll your hands mechanically until your silent message becomes loud and clear.

73. **The Attention-Getter** - Whistle at someone too far away to start a conversation with. When they turn to look, send it.

74. **The Chainsaw** - Act like you're pull-starting a chainsaw, then give them the wide-open throttle.

75. **The Free Throw** - Form and follow-through are key.

76. **The Backflip** - Turn around and say "backflip" as you send them one from behind. Requires a LOT less exertion than a real backflip.

77. ***Pushes Glasses Up***

78. **The Eyebrow Straightener** - Middle finger eyebrow iron.

79. **The Nose Picker** - Eew. But it's fun to pretend you're buried to the second knuckle if you're good at sneaking your finger open as you pull it away.

80. **The Lawn Sprinkler** - Like the dance move, only better. "Ch-ch-ch-ch..."

81. **The Ear-a-Tater** - Pop those ear spuds loose with the longest finger on either hand.

82. **"The Plane! The Plane!"** - "Look! Up there!"

83. **The Toothpick** - Trust me, that middle fingernail can dig just about anything out from between those choppers.

84. **The Double-Digit Nipple Rub** - Sell it, big fella!

85. **The Pickpocket** - Pretend you're taking something out of someone's pocket. When you get busted, show them what you stole.

86. **The Shotput** – Spin like you're in the pit and let it fly. Try to get good loft by stretching the follow-through.

87. **Resting Bitchfinger** - If the creeper at the next table can't keep their eyes to themselves, send them an inconspicuous (yet constant) greeting as you carry on your conversation.

88. **The Pluck Yew** - Act like you're pulling back a bow, and when you let it fly, let it fly!

89. **The Belly Button Digger** - Finds lint, bubble gum, lost change, etc.

90. **The Extra Terrestrial** - It's easy to re-create famous movie scenes involving fingers.

91. **The Stir Stick** - Pretend you're using your little friend to stir your drink.

92. **The F*ckunicorn** – Holding a finger to look like a horn, say, "Oh look! It's a..."

93. **The Hot Potato** - Pretend you're juggling a hot potato, making a finger as you catch it, then toss it to your friends.

94. **The Motorcyclist** - Grab both handlebars and twist a grip. Vroom! Vroom!

95. **The Unsend** - If you notice someone you hadn't seen, morph your finger back into your fist and roll that baby into a thumbs-up with a smile...

96. **The Doggy Paddle** - Fingers out as you swim around.

97. **The Signal Man** - Every good crane operator needs good signals. Mix things up!

98. **The Trash Poker** - Pretend your favorite finger is that old stick you'd use to pick up something nasty to throw it away.

99. **The Second-Hand Storyteller** - "I heard a story about an old man in a factory who would walk up and ask if people got one of THESE yet today..."

100. **Throw the Book at Them** - Pop the question, and if they act offended, show them what you're reading.

101. **The Graceful Exit** - "Oh, and ONE more thing... Have a great day!"

Got your own unique idea on how to pop the question?

I'm planning on making a flip (pun intended) calendar when I get to 365 ideas.

If you'd like a chance to see your idea in print, send your submissions to brandy@autoworkertales.com with "Ways to Pop the Question" in the subject line for the opportunity to win a free book and/or calendar.

Where to Next?

"**Did You Get One of THESE Yet Today**" is book one of the Autoworker Tales series.

I plan to add at least four more to this collection.

If you'd like to be notified when the other books are released, go to www.autoworkertales.com for more information.

A brief overview of the books and what they're about:

"**They're Just Car Parts**" – Production workers, industrial situations, and plant life in general.

"**Best Job in the Plant**" – Plant life from a skilled trades perspective.

"**A Peek at the Undercarriage**" – Stories you shouldn't tell grandma at bedtime.

"**Planes, Trains, and Autoworkers**" – Autoworker hobbies, interests, and ways to pass the time.

Made in the USA
Columbia, SC
07 December 2023

28006873R00137